Abou...

...rrie Bright is a self-confessed bookaholic and magazine addict. She was born in Wales but later moved to England and settled in South Yorkshire. She felt a bit strange as the 'new girl in school' and would escape between the covers of a book whenever possible. Characters created by E. Nesbit, N. Streatfield and E. Goudge were her friends.

As a teenager she would go round to her (real) best friend's and read all her magazines one after another. They tried out every top tip and fashion feature possible – Carrie seems to remember mixing up a mud-coloured lipstick, wearing fashion-victim clothes and wishing she had some of the worries she read about in the problem pages! Going to a girls' school meant she could only dream of romance – which probably inspired some of the *Maddy* stories.

Carrie works part time as a children's librarian. You visit her website at www.carriebright.co.uk to find our more about *Maddy*, and also about *Jamie B*, a series of books Carrie wrote under her other name, Ceri Worman.

With thanks again to the pupils of Westborough High School, Dewsbury, who read the manuscript and gave me enthusiastic and constructive comments: Kiran Akhtar, Shannon Barrowcliffe, Zeba Hussain, Faaiza Khan, Asma Patel, Zakirrah Razaq, Zara Rauf, Neelam Riaz, Kiran Sadiq, Sanha Saleem and to Fiona Bruce for making it possible.

ORCHARD BOOKS
338 Euston Road, London NW1 3BH
Orchard Books Australia
Level 17/207 Kent Street, Sydney, NSW 2000

ISBN: 978 1 84616 328 9

First published in 2008 by Orchard Books
A paperback original

Text © Ceri Worman 2008
Illustrations © Jessie Eckel 2008

The right of Ceri Worman to be identified as
the author of this work has been asserted by her
in accordance with the Copyright, Designs and Patents Act, 1988.

1 3 5 7 9 10 8 6 4 2
Printed in Great Britain

Orchard Books is a division of Hachette Children's Books,
an Hachette Livre UK company.

www.hachettelivre.co.uk

Maddy

GOTHIC GODDESS

destiny, darkness and deadly drama!

ORCHARD BOOKS

Hi, it's Maddy Blue here and I'm a total mag-hag – addicted to magazines!

When I'm feeling mad, sad or bad I buy myself one, crawl between the bright, shiny pages and get lost forever. (Mad's note: Some people wish I would...)

If my life was a magazine would it be a girly-world one full of plastic-fantastic fun? Or an indie title full of destiny, darkness and deadly drama?

You be the judge. Here's my life in a magazine. (Well, kind of.) I cut up some Gothic comics and used them to customise the story. Then I added some dark drawings and Mad notes.

Hope you enjoy it!

Maddy x

The World's Top Teen Magazine!

written, edited, designed and published by

Maddy Blue

Issue No. 2:

Gothic Goddess!

WHAT'S INSIDE?

1

STARGAZER

Spectacular surprises for Leos this month!

Venus is rising and love is in the air...
If you're single, you're going to meet the soul mate you've been searching for.

You've got a hot date with Fate, so don't fight it!

'Where is she, Scott? Why isn't she here?' I say as we get to the school gates on Monday morning. The last thing she said was, '*See you next week, same time, same place*,' so why isn't she here?

'Don't worry about it.' Scott tries to sound cool but I can see that even he looks a bit rattled. 'Things happen. She might be late or—'

The bell rings and interrupts his attempt at soothing words.

'Well, there's nothing we can do about it right now,' he says as we hurry through the main entrance and plunge into the corridor. 'I'll talk to you at break, OK?'

He's right, there's nothing we can do about it, but that doesn't stop me from worrying.

Things haven't been going well at home for Starr. Her Mum took off quite suddenly to London and Starr went to visit her. She didn't return my calls yesterday and I'm desperate to find out what happened.

Mondays are the best time to catch up because we both have the same lessons all morning and can gossip without driving Scott mad. Today's different – no Starr, so no *giggly girly goss*.

I feel like a *Lost Soul* – which is the name of my new mag tucked safely away in my bag. Everyone else is in their own groups and gangs while I push through the crowds all alone.

Suddenly I get this strange, hollow feeling in the pit of my stomach, like a warning.

(*Mad's note: Either that or you forgot to eat your breakfast.*)

At least I can read the 'Stargazer' page at break time – take a sneaky peek into the future and find out what's happening to Starr...

❤ ★ ♡

'What a load of rubbish!' I say, slamming *Lost Soul* down on the desk two hours later.

We're stuck in a hot, smelly, overcrowded classroom because it's raining outside. I'm in a mood.

'It's so disappointing! D'you think I could take it back and get a refund?'

'Why did you buy it in the first place?' Scott asks.

Then he looks more closely at the black and silver cover. It's scattered with moons and stars and the weird title, *Lost Soul*, is written in strange loopy letters. 'This isn't the one you normally buy, is it?'

Scott isn't a fan of my mags so I'm amazed he even noticed. 'No, but I was getting sick of all that plastic-fantastic, girly-world stuff. This one looked different. And guess what? I didn't even choose it – *it* chose *me*.'

Scott gives me a look. 'What – did it fly off the shelf or something?'

'Yes – it kind of leapt at me and fluttered down to the floor – *spooky!*' I open it up to demonstrate. 'It was flapping its dark, paper wings like a bat out of hell.'

'Really?'

'Of course! So I had to buy it. Don't you think *Lost Soul* sounds kind of dark and prophetic?'

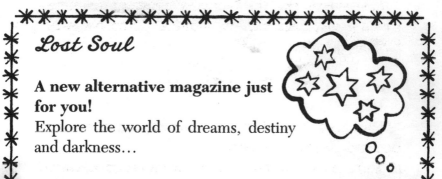

Lost Soul

A new alternative magazine just for you!
Explore the world of dreams, destiny and darkness…

Unleash your magic powers and let your spirit soar!
(Special introductory price)

He takes it from me and flicks through a few pages. 'So what's wrong with it, then? I thought you said it was rubbish.'

'Yeah, "*Explore the world of dreams, destiny and darkness...*" It sounds deep, intense and soulful but it's not. It's completely silly and shallow. *Look...*'

I point to the 'Stargazer' page and Scott reads. '*Hmmm, it says luurve is in the air... What's wrong with that?*'

I hold up my fingers and start counting. '*One* – that's what they *always* say. *Two* – where's the stuff about friendship? I want to know what's going to happen to Starr! *Three* – I'm going to meet my *soul mate*? Have you looked round the class recently? Where is he then?'

Scott follows my eyes and we watch what the boys are up to. They're either stuffing their faces with food, glued to computer screens or playing football with empty plastic bottles.

'Soul mates? I don't *think* so,' I say, turning away in disgust.

'"*Stargazer*"?' Scott's laughing now. '"*Venus is rising!*" ...Why do you even read this trash, anyway? It's superstition and speculation. Stick to science – you know it makes sense.'

He hands me his big, thick science textbook.

'Yeah, thanks,' I say, flicking through pages of diagrams and data. 'Just what I always wanted.'

Scott rolls up my nice, new, shiny magazine into a tight tube. 'So I'll bin this for you then, shall I?' he says, getting up and walking away.

'No, wait!'

I grab his boring old textbook and hold it up high, cupping my hand like a megaphone. *'SCOTT, PUT THE MAG DOWN OR THE SCIENCE BOOK GETS IT!'*

Suddenly I'm feeling all protective about *Lost Soul*. Maybe it's too soon to pass a final opinion – I haven't even read most of it yet.

'I knew it!' he laughs. 'Once a mag-hag, *always* a mag-hag! OK, OK, I give up.'

I hand over his book and he surrenders my mag. Then I smooth it out and open up the silvery pages, reading the stars again, just in case there was something I missed.

'*Soul mate... Spectacular surprises...*' If only it were true...

Suddenly the lights flicker on and off. Lightning flashes outside, followed by a spectacular crash of thunder.

Booommm!!!

Half the class rush to the window to see what's happening, then someone screams – a loud, bloodcurdling sound that chills the blood...

'AAAAAAaaaghhhhhhhhhhhhhhhhhhh!!!'

(Mad's note: OK, true confession. It's me – but I'm not the only one.)

'Scary!' I grab Scott's arm. 'It's still rumbling and grumbling out there like a huge, horrible, hairy monster!'

'Yeah, yeah, that's right,' he says, sarcastically. 'Either that or it's a build-up of positive and negative electrical charges... They meet to create a bolt of electricity and a shockwave of sound known as thunder.'

But I'm not even listening. The lights flicker on again and something compels me to turn around.

Standing in the doorway is a tall, dark, mysterious stranger, dressed all in black.

He looks deep, intense and soulful...

I can tell by:

a. His deep, intense and soulful hairstyle
b. His deep, intense and soulful clothes
c. His deep, intense and soulful eyes

Everyone else is still looking out of the window. No one sees him except me. Our eyes meet and he slowly raises one finger in a signal to keep quiet.

This isn't a problem – I'm speechless with shock anyway.

The shock that you get when lightning strikes and your soul mate walks into the room.

He moves silently like a shadow and pins something on the notice board at the back of the class.

Then he crosses the room again, pausing briefly at the door to give me a wink.

By the time I can speak he's gone.

2

PSYCHIC
POWERS

Do you have a sixth sense?

✳ *Can you guess what your friend is going to say next?*

✳ *Do you sometimes know who it is when the phone rings?*

✳ *Can you send a secret mind-message?*

Take our simple telepathy test to find out...

'Spectacular surprise,' I whisper in Scott's ear.

'Yes, nature's very own firework display,' he agrees, his eyes still fixed on the brooding sky outside.

'No, Scott. Something *amazing* happened, just like "Stargazer" predicted! A mysterious stranger appeared in the thunderstorm. He pinned something on the notice board and then vanished...'

'Into thin air?'

'Out of the door, you idiot! Don't you believe me?'

He crosses his arms in front of him. 'Nope, I'm a scientist. Show me the evidence.'

I drag him over to the board and we look at the poster. A black bat hovers over thick, Olde English lettering:

Lady and the Vamp
A Gothic Romance

Screenplay by Caspar LeStrange

Auditions: Tuesday
Place: The Olde Annexe
Time: Twilight (after school)

Dare to be there!
(Rehearsals at school. Will be filmed in a mystery location.)

'The Olde Annexe? Isn't that where the arty types hang out? So your mystery guy's a poser from Performing Arts looking for recruits. Not much of a surprise after all.'

The bell goes for the end of break. Scott turns away but I stay where I am – staring at the poster.

He's wrong – this is a surprise…a spectacular surprise.

Love is in the air and I've just been struck by a thunderbolt!

How romantic! Did the mysterious Goth write the screenplay? I bet he did. He looks so soulful, tortured and creative.

Caspar LeStrange.

He's the one. I'm sure.

As soon as he walked through the door I knew it.

Caspar LeStrange.

He looked as if he was born on the storm… He looked like the Prince of Darkness and I want to be his slave forever!

Now even looking at his name makes my spine tingle.

Caspar LeStrange…

The only way I'll find out for sure is by going to the audition – but there's no way I'd dare go alone…

'Come on, Maddy. It's maths next, hurry up!'

I tear my eyes away from the poster and follow Scott down the corridor.

Five minutes later I'm in a fix. The figures on the page are dancing around in front of me making no sense at all.

How can I concentrate on maths at a time like this?

If only Starr was here. I really need to have a serious heart-to-heart with her. Scott's my best mate, but I can't talk to him about love!

Anyway, maths is one of his favourite lessons. He'd just tell me to shut up and add up – or multiply, or divide, or whatever we're supposed to be doing.

This is serious girl-talk and I need Starr. She'd understand, I'm sure. She'd come with me to the audition. She'd prop me up when I'm shaking with nerves and embarrassment. That's what friends are for, but...where is she?

I put my hand up to ask for help with my maths and while I'm waiting, an idea pops into my mind like telepathic toast.

Why not test my psychic powers and send Starr a mind-message?

Luckily, I just read a feature about it in *Lost Soul*, so I know exactly what to do...

Top three telepathy tips!
(Messaging for free – all you need is an open mind)

1. Think of nothing else – block out any distractions around you.
2. Keep the message simple.
3. Say the name of the person you want to reach.

I close my eyes and concentrate really hard, repeating the same message over and over in my head:

Come back Starr, Come back Starr, Come back Starr...

Then I'm sure I can hear her calling my name:

Maddy, MADDY, MADDY!

I open my eyes, expecting to see Starr right in front of me...

Nooooo!!!

My maths teacher is up-close and far-too-personal and everyone is watching.

'Maddy...Maddy Blue – are you asleep?'

'Er, no Sir. I was just, um, resting my eyes,' I say, as someone makes a loud snoring noise behind me.

'Hmm, well make sure you get to bed early tonight,' he says, turning to look at the blank page in my maths book. 'Now, what's the problem?'

But I don't get the chance to tell him, because just then the door opens and Starr walks in.

I can't believe it, the message worked! Starr has appeared out of nowhere and it's all because I gave her a psychic phone-call...a telepathic text!

How many other paranormal powers do I have inside, just waiting to be discovered?

Starr smiles at me and then slips quickly into an empty seat at the front. She looks as if she doesn't want a fuss so I switch my mind-messager off. We can catch up for real at lunchtime.

Sir goes over to her and they talk in hushed whispers while I go back to my work. Using those psychic powers must have spring-cleaned my brain because all of a sudden the maths looks easy...

(Mad's note: Maths = easy? That's not just spooky, it's über-creepy.)

As soon as the lesson ends I rush over to Starr.

'So, you got it then – the message?' I say enthusiastically.

'Yeah, sorry I didn't answer. You know how it is...'

I'm amazed at how casual she sounds. *How many mind-messages does Starr get every day?* I wonder. Maybe there's a whole psychic-sisterhood out there that I know nothing about...

'My phone was switched off because Honey really needed to talk. Then when she did, there was so much for me to think about I just needed some space. I only picked up your message this morning.'

'Yes, don't worry – I understand,' I say as it dawns on me that she's talking about an actual message I left on her phone.

Suddenly all this psychic stuff seems trivial compared to what Starr's going through. I don't need to be clairvoyant to see how worried she looks.

It's strange because she seemed so glamorous, dropping into our boring world after living in Spain for a year. Her mum, Honey, is an ex-model and her dad, Matt, is a musician. They bought Bar Salsa in the centre of town and I thought she was so lucky to have parents like that, compared to my boring lot.

But I soon found out her life isn't as glam as it seemed. Her parents are always arguing, although Starr told me this is the first time Honey has actually walked out.

Scott joins us and gets straight to the point. 'So how was your trip? How's Honey? Did she come back with you?'

Starr shakes her head. She looks around and signals that she doesn't want to talk in front of the others.

We hang around for a bit while everyone rushes off to eat. When the classroom empties it goes very quiet at first and no one says anything. Scott has his nose in a book and I doodle a heart on my pencil case. Starr stands by the window, looking out at the rain.

When she finally speaks her voice sounds flat, like she's reading from an autocue. 'Honey's not coming back – ever.' She tries to smile but doesn't quite succeed. I know she's upset but is doing her best not to show it. 'She wants to start a new life in London—'

'Why? You've only been here a few months!' I can't help interrupting because it seems so unfair. I know Starr's fed up of moving around and she was just settling down here. Besides, I was getting used to having a girl as a best friend – as well as Scott, of course.

'She says it's Matt's fault the business failed in Spain and he dragged her to Westfield. She told me she's not going to rot away in this dump. She wants the bright lights.'

'Dump?' I say, suddenly feeling defensive about my home town.

'Her words, not mine,' Starr says. 'Matt loves it. He grew up here – he hates city life.'

'So you're moving to London?' Scott states the obvious conclusion. We all know that Honey will make things very difficult if she doesn't get her own way.

'I don't know.' She shakes her head and looks out of the window again as if gathering herself for her next words.

'Honey's going to divorce Matt. She wants me to go and live with her. She didn't shout or try to force me to stay...she probably knows I'd do the opposite if she did. She just told me to take some time to decide for myself.'

Scott and I look at each other and that hollow feeling I had this morning comes back again.

'Are you going?' I ask, as gently as I can.

Starr shrugs. She turns her pale face to us and when she speaks her voice is a whisper. 'My choice – stay with my dad or leave with my mum. How do you decide a thing like that?'

3

THE GREAT
FATE DEBATE

Fate vs. free will — what rules your life?

Are you a Mystic Miss, an Open-Minder or a No-Nonsense Nerd?

Answer our quick quiz and find out where you fit in the Great Fate Debate.

Scott's the first to speak and when he does, he says all the right things. 'You don't have to decide right now, Starr. Give yourself some time. This choice will change your life. You can't make it overnight, can you?'

She shakes her head. 'No – Honey drives me mad sometimes but she's got so many plans for the future. She says living in London's going to open lots of doors for us...'

'And Matt, will he carry on living here?' I ask, hoping she hasn't made up her mind already.

'Yes, he told me this morning. We might have to move out of Bar Salsa, though. Honey's got the business brain and I don't know if he'll manage.'

'Maybe he could earn a living as a musician?' I say. Every time I see him he's strumming his guitar. When he sings you believe that music makes everything right in the world. 'He's got talent – he writes all his own songs, doesn't he?'

'*Mmm*, sometimes – Honey says he's just a dreamer. But at least staying with him means I'd still see you two… If I go with her then—'

'London's not so far on the train,' Scott interrupts. 'You've got to think of yourself here, Starr. What's best for you in the long run. Why don't you write all the plus and minus points against each option? Then you can look at things logically.'

'Ye-es…' Starr says, but she doesn't look convinced.

As for me, I'm shocked.

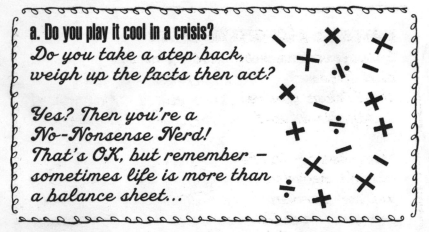

a. Do you play it cool in a crisis?
Do you take a step back, weigh up the facts then act?

Yes? Then you're a No-Nonsense Nerd! That's OK, but remember – sometimes life is more than a balance sheet…

Forget what I said about Scott saying all the right things. At first I thought he was being sensible, but now…

'Scott – Starr can't decide like that! What about Fate and...*feelings*? Where do they come in?'

'But that's my point, Maddy. You have to forget your feelings and look at things logically. And what's *Fate* got to do with it?'

'Well, I think Starr's meant to stay in Westfield for some reason that...that's yet to be revealed.' I turn to Starr for support. 'After all, Fate brought you here, didn't it?'

She smiles, 'Actually, it was an aeroplane that brought me back from Spain. Then a car got me here...'

And now they're both laughing and I join in too because it's great to see Starr looking happy for a few seconds.

'Oh, I can't explain it properly,' I say, pulling out *Lost Soul* and waving it at them in my defence. 'But there's something about Fate in here and it really makes you think...'

b. Do you trust in Fate and go with the flow?
Is your life run by Astro, Tarot and Cosmo?
Yes? Then you're a Mystic Miss!

Your head's in the clouds, but don't get too carried away...or you'll end up as a Mystic Mess!

Scott checks his watch. 'Much as I'd love to carry on this Great Fate Debate, I have to go and help out at the computer club. I haven't got time to eat now, so save me some food and I'll catch you both later?'

He heads for the door, adding, 'Can you get out your crystal ball and tell me what's on the menu today then, Maddy?'

'Why yes my dear... Eye of Newt and Toe of Frog,' I say in a witchy voice, waving my arms around. *'And I'll save you a large portion with extra eyes.'*

c. If life's hard do you consult your head, heart *and* crystal ball?

Do you talk with friends, read your stars and take time to think? If the answer's yes, you're an Open-Minder.

You listen to common sense and cosmic sense. That's all good — but sometimes a bit confusing!

When he's gone Starr flicks through my magazine, saying 'Haven't seen this one before. Is it any good?'

'It's *spooktacular*!' I say. 'Honestly Starr, ever since I got this mag some weird things have happened. Not in a kooky-spooky way but in a dramatic-destiny kind of way...'

'Really?' she looks up, intrigued. 'Why, what have I missed?'

'Well there was this thunderstorm and this gorgeous boy appeared. Ooh, he was a vision in boho-black and—'

Then I stop. What am I doing? Here's Starr tearing her heart out about her mum and dad splitting up and I'm telling her about my latest crush?

How crass!
How shallow!
How plastic!
When will I ever learn?

'Go on,' Starr says, 'you can't stop now.'

'No,' I shake my head. 'It's not important. What's important is you and your future. That's what we should be talking about.'

'No, I've done nothing but think and cry for the last two days. Now I feel numb – I'm desperate to talk about something else. Go on, tell me everything.'

I give her a hug because she's so brave and such a good friend. 'OK, well according to my mag I had a date with Fate and *HE* turned up right on time...'

'Who did? Who's *he*?'

'Oh, I'm not sure what he's called,' I say vaguely.

Why can't I speak his name? It's like I'm hugging it to me like a sacred secret.

This must be Love with a capital L!

(*Mad's note: Or PSYCHO with a capital P-S-Y-C-H-O.*)

'But if I'm going to see him again, I need your help...' I continue.

'Yes, OK. What did you have in mind?'

'Well he put up this poster about a film he's making – *Lady and the Vamp*—'

'Sounds a bit Gothic.'

'*Omigoth!* He definitely is. I think I'm turning a bit that way myself – discovering my dark side. Ever since I picked up this mag it's bringing out the vamp in me. That's why I want to go to the tryouts for the film. But I daren't go alone...'

I pause dramatically and Starr comes in, right on cue. 'Don't worry, I'll come with you.'

'*Thankyouthankyouthankyou!* But are you sure? I mean with things as they are at home?'

'Yes, this'll help take my mind off all that! Anyway, it sounds like fun – not that I'm a closet Goth myself. Although I do quite like their fashion-sense.'

'Well, wait till you see him,' I say breathlessly. 'He's so unique, but what's going to make him look at a loser like me?'

'Maddy, you're not a loser. If it's meant to be, then it'll happen – just relax and go with the flow.'

'Hmmm, I'm not sure... What if I help things along a bit? Let's call it cosmic insurance cover. That wouldn't do any harm would it?'

'Sorry, you've lost me. What are you talking about?'

(Mad's note: When in doubt - whip your mag out!)

I find *Lost Soul* and flick it open, skimming down the contents page.

'There!' I say, slamming it on the desk and pointing to my fiendish plan...

'Love Spells,' Starr reads aloud. 'See next page...'

4

LOVE SPELLS

LOVE SPELLS

Casting spells is simply a way of spelling out to the universe what you want to happen.

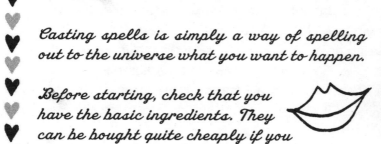

Before starting, check that you have the basic ingredients. They can be bought quite cheaply if you know where to look...

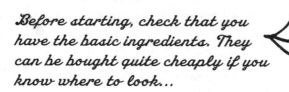

'Scott, you don't have to come if you don't want to,' I say as we weave our way through market stalls after school.

'You're right, I don't have to and I don't want to but I will come with you – to protect you.'

'Oh, come on, we're big girls now, we can look after ourselves,' Starr laughs.

'Yes, maybe *you* can, but Maddy has been known to get carried away before now.'

Scott gives me a look and I stick my tongue out at him. That's the problem with being friends forever – he knows me too well.

'I just don't want you wasting your money at this *Mystic Market*, that's all,' he adds. 'Who knows what you might buy?'

'We're just looking for some basic spell-making stuff! Oh, and maybe something to give us a touch of Gothic glamour before the tryouts tomorrow,' I say.

'*Hmm*, I rest my case. Why don't you just trust your own talent?'

'I would if I had some... Ooh look, there it is!'

In front of us are two stalls. One has a sign saying *Mystic Market* with a rainbow of colours arcing across it. The other has a sign saying *Bizarre Bazaar* in silver Gothic letters on a black background.

These two stalls are basically the extent of the Mystic Market. It might be small but it looks magically massive to me.

'Oh, don't you just want everything?' I say, looking at the crystals, candles, joss sticks and little bottles of mysterious oils.

'Better start with what's on the list first,' Starr reminds me.

I sneak a peek at *Lost Soul*, turning to the spells.

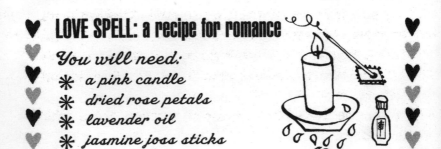

♥ LOVE SPELL: a recipe for romance

You will need:
* ✳ *a pink candle*
* ✳ *dried rose petals*
* ✳ *lavender oil*
* ✳ *jasmine joss sticks*

Starr helps me find the ingredients and we hand them over to the girl running the stall.

Her name badge reads Raven and with her dark velvet clothes, long black hair and silver jewellery, she's got real *Gothitude*!

'Perfect ingredients for a love spell,' she says, wrapping them in black tissue paper, tied with a silver ribbon.

'Love spell? I thought you said it was a good luck spell, so you'd both get a part in the film,' Scott hisses.

'Oh, er...fancy that! Must be the same ingredients,' I mutter.

(Mad's note: OK, so it's an un-Gothic white lie, but I suspect Scott wouldn't approve of me luring a lad with my love charms!)

'And look over here, it's all Goth-tastic!' I say, changing the subject and moving to the *Bizarre Bazaar* stall.

We stand there admiring the *Cute Coffin Cosmetic Cases*, *Beautiful Batwing Bangles* and *Striking Skull Earrings*.

'Charming,' Scott says, rolling his eyes.

'And there's *Lost Soul* in that pile of Gothic comics and mystic mags,' I add, pointing at the back of the stall. 'See? That's destiny – I was definitely drawn here by a cosmic thread!'

I pick it up and shriek with surprise. '*Omigoth* – it's Issue Number Two and it's got a free bottle of nail polish, *Back-to-Black*! Can you save it for me?' I ask Raven, who's moved across to this stall now. 'I get my allowance on Saturday and—'

'Let me pay,' Starr interrupts, reaching across with the money.

Let her?

'Well, if you insist.' I say, grabbing the mag and hugging it to me.

'Are you sure?' Scott asks. 'It looks quite expensive.'

'Yeah,' I squeak, feeling guilty and putting it down again. I stroke the cover sadly. 'Scott's right, it's too much...'

'Don't worry, I've got plenty of cash,' Starr says. 'Honey gave me some yesterday and then Matt did too – it's either guilt or a bribe, who knows? You might as well make use of it.'

She hands over the money but I feel terrible. It's like I'm spending her wages of sorrow, and what kind of person would do that?

I'm just about to refuse when Raven speaks. 'There's a limited offer with this, too. Do you want this sample-pack *Back-to-Black* hair dye?'

'*No!*' '*Yes!*' Scott and I say together.

Scott looks at me. 'Maddy, you don't need it. Your hair's fine as it is!'

'Yeah, but we really need to Goth up a bit for tomorrow. What d'you think, Starr?'

'Give it a try,' Starr says, shaking her lovely long blonde hair, 'but it's not for me.' I can see she's got a point but with my ginger frizz there's nothing to lose.

'It's only a wash-out dye, so it won't last long,' Raven says, smiling. 'Go on – live a little!'

'Or dye a little,' Scott mutters, shaking his head at me.

'That's a bit harsh!' I say as we make our way back to the High Street.

'I meant *d-y-e*,' Scott says, 'but I really don't think it's a good idea for the two of you to dabble in the Black Arts.'

'We're not!' I say. 'We're dabbling in black nail polish, that's all! Don't be so serious, Scott, it's only a bit of fun.'

He doesn't answer and stares ahead with a strange look on his face. I follow his eyes and see why. There's a ladder propped up against a building and we're going to have to pass it. If we carry on as we are, we'll walk right underneath.

'Ladder alert,' I say. 'Bad Luck – step aside!'

Starr and I move over to avoid it but Scott carries on walking straight ahead.

'Don't, Scott! Anything could happen—'

But he's already through it and out the other side. 'It's a miracle!' he says, holding his arms out. 'Look, I'm still alive!'

'OK, OK, so maybe you think it's a silly superstition, but why tempt Fate?' I say.

'To prove how stupid it is. You just like spooking yourselves! My mum's exactly the same.'

'Is she?' I say in surprise. 'You mean Hyacinth Lord, hard-working nurse and respectable churchgoer? She's into magic and making spells?'

'Well not exactly...but when I was little she used to scare me and my cousins half to death.' He puts on a deep, scary voice. 'Spooky stories about *duppies and jumbies and the obeah man!*'

'Who?' Starr looks confused.

'They're ghosts and spirits from the Caribbean,' Scott explains. 'Oh, and another thing she always tells us, "*What goes around comes around*". So you must take care. Don't meddle with magic – that's a warning!'

GOOD SPELLING GUIDE

Remember: magic is an energy source – it will return to you threefold.

Think of this before you cast a spell.

'Hang on – you think magic is airy-fairy nonsense!' I say to Scott, wagging my finger at him. 'So how can you warn us against something you don't believe in? That's not logical!'

Even Scott has to smile at this.

Yes! One paranormal point to me!

I mean, what can possibly go wrong with a love spell?

5

SPELL-CASTING

Before casting your spell, read these words and heed them well...

True love comes as a surprise
True love lies beyond the eyes
To find the half to make you whole
Look deep within your heart and soul

Open your heart to love that's true
Call your soul mate close to you

Starr agrees to come home with me after the shopping trip but Scott says he's got more important things to do now, i.e. homework.

I ask you – how can that be more important than casting a love spell?

As soon as we open the door two strange creatures leap out at us from the gloomy hallway. One is small, furry and licky, the other small, squirmy and sticky.

(Mad's note: No, not an evil hobbit and a spiteful sprite, just Chester the dog and Max my little brother.)

'Max, *gerroff!*' I say. 'What have you been eating? It's everywhere!'

'Making fairy cakes with Mum,' Max says proudly, skittering off back to the kitchen.

'Chester, get down!' I grab his collar to stop him jumping up at Starr. He's barking with excitement as if he hasn't seen a human in a million years.

'That's it, good dog,' she says calmly, stroking his head.

'Oh, why do I have a fat smelly dog instead of a sleek black cat?' I moan. 'Apparently they're much more useful as assistants for spell-casting.'

'*Hmm*, some matches would be useful, too – for the candle and joss sticks.'

She's right. Even would-be witches have to take care of the practical side of life.

I sneak into the kitchen wondering how to explain things to Mum but I needn't have worried – she's far too busy to care what I'm doing. She's up to her elbows in a bowl of cake mix, trying to control Max, who's stirring and splashing like a mad magician's assistant.

'Starr's with me, we'll be in my room,' I say, opening a drawer and pocketing a little box of matches.

'That's nice, love,' she says without even turning round to look at me. 'Max – go easy on the milk, we don't want soggy fairy cakes, do we?'

'Soggy fairies! Soggy fairies!' Max chants as I disappear into the hall.

'*Bless!*' Starr smiles, fondly. 'He's so sweet!'

I pull a face. 'No, he's not – he's a half-crazed hobgoblin!

But at least he's busy so he won't pester us for a while.'

We go into my room and I lock my door for extra spell-casting security.

Starr sits in a chair, opens up *Lost Soul* and starts reading while I lay out the ingredients on my bed.

'OK, there's the candle, oil, rose petals and joss sticks. What happens now?'

'Are you going to do the spell skyclad?'

'Skyclad? What's that?'

Starr starts giggling. 'Er, birthday suit, undressed...*naked.*'

'Oh no, that's *über-weird*! Are you serious?'

'Yes, it says here you can either do it skyclad or in an appropriate robe.'

I grab my dressing gown from the back of the door and wrap it round me. It's a bit lumpy-bumpy over my school uniform but better than the alternative.

'There, what next?'

Starr reads aloud from the mag. '*Light the candle and joss sticks to create a dreamy, scented atmosphere. Then sprinkle the rose petals with lavender oil for loved-up vibes.*'

I strike a match and light the candle and joss sticks. It's getting dark outside and Starr switches off the light.

'Shall I draw the curtains?' I say, moving to the window. For some reason I'm whispering now.

'No, it says that the best time to do this is by the light of a new moon,' Starr whispers back.

I can see a fingernail of moon chalked in the twilight sky. 'Perfect,' I breathe. 'What next?'

'Simply say this spell to attract your loved one to you.'

She hands over the mag and I mumble the words under my breath over and over.

All the time I'm thinking of Caspar LeStrange and the way I felt when our eyes met – the day that thunder rumbled outside and lightning split the sky.

The day that changed my life forever.

When I know the spell by heart I stand up, sprinkle oil on the rose petals and start chanting.

*'Whisper love spells to the air
So they will carry everywhere
One alone your words will hear
One alone will then draw near...'*

THUMP!!!

Suddenly there's a loud thud at the door that makes me yelp in surprise.

Starr looks at me wide-eyed.

Has something gone wrong?

Have I called up evil spirits by mistake?

'Maddy, Maddy – come and see my fairy cakes!'

Max's voice is high and excited. He's jiggling the door handle and ruining the mystic mood.

'Go away, Max, I'm busy!' I say, sharply.

Then I hear a snort from the corner of the room. Starr's shoulders are shaking and she looks as if she's going to explode. I can't believe it.

'Stop laughing, Starr! This is serious magic – I want it to work!'

'Sorry, sorry,' she says, taking out a tissue and blowing her nose. 'It was just the look on your face, that's all. Go on.'

We hear Max's footsteps go downstairs and I try to get back into the spell-casting zone, but it's hopeless. Even wafting a joss stick around witchily doesn't work.

'It's gone,' I say. 'The spell's broken and we've lost the magic!'

'Why don't you say the words, anyway – maybe you can bring it back?' Starr says hopefully.

'OK,' I sigh. 'Here goes…

Rose and jasmine, fire and air
Bring to me the one who cares –
Let the new moon be my guide
Sending true love to my side.'

But Caspar's face has disappeared. I slump on the bed feeling totally dispirited.

'Don't stop yet!' Starr says, looking at my magazine. 'It says here you must always seal a spell with these words to the universe.'

She holds out *Lost Soul* and I read,

*For the Highest Good of All
And It Harm None. So Be It.*

We bow our heads solemnly, waiting for the universe to receive my spellbinding...

'Maddy! Starr! I'm back – and I've got fairy cakes for you!'

Max thumps on the door again, Starr collapses into a fit of giggles and I groan. I know he won't give up until we've answered him.

'Stop banging,' I shout. 'Just wait a minute!'

I blow out the candle and joss sticks, unlock the door and open it a tiny bit. A little fist reaches through, clutching a lumpy cake in a frilly case.

'Here you go! One for you...' The fist disappears and comes back again, 'and one for Starr.'

'Thanks Max, that's lovely. Now you go downstairs and we'll be down soon, OK?'

'OK!'

I close the door and switch on the light.

'D'you think the spell worked?' Starr asks, taking a cake and prodding it curiously.

'Not really,' I say. 'It felt right at first – a definite magical connection – but then I got cut off. I'll try again when Max is in bed.'

'Shame I can't stay that long,' Starr says. 'We could have another go, but I promised Matt I wouldn't be late. Someone's got to make sure he eats. All he does is sit strumming his guitar, singing tragic love songs.'

I nod, knowing it would take more than an *Über-Strong Love Spell* to bring Honey and Matt back together again.

'But I've just got enough time to do your nails,' she says, opening up the bottle of *Back-to-Black*.

She sweeps dark stripes across my perfectly pink pearlies, adding, '*Um*, are you going to eat Max's cakes?'

I shake my head. 'No, they look disgusting! We'll just have to pretend we did. It's either that or risk food poisoning – and I'm not ready to die yet. That comes later tonight!'

'Sorry?'

'The black hair dye – remember? I'm dye-ing tonight.' I waggle a handful of blackened claws at her. 'Tomorrow you won't even know me – I'm going to be reborn as Lady Madalena – Gothic Goddess!'

6

DISCOVER THE
GODDESS INSIDE YOU!

DISCOVER THE GODDESS INSIDE YOU!

Thousands of years ago goddesses were worshipped for their beauty, wisdom and special powers.

Read on to find out how to capture their divine qualities for yourself...

What in Goth's name is a Gothic Goddess anyway?

To be honest I have no idea, but if Caspar LeStrange is going to fall under my spell, I have to find out fast!

He's not the type to go for a fat, frizzy nobody like me. Somehow I have to reinvent myself as someone dark, mysterious and fascinating – a Gothic Goddess to match Caspar the Gothic God...

It's not going to be easy but we are fated to be together – it's written in the stars (or at least in the pages of my magazine). Destiny demands it and that gives me strength.

After Starr leaves I lock myself in my room and lose myself between the pages of *Lost Soul*:

Dress for destiny!   **Spells for all occasions!**

Gothic magic!   **REVEAL YOUR INNER GODDESS!**

The power of dreams!   Mystic make-up!

I emerge from the magical pages feeling totally mesmerised.

Lost Soul has become a part of me. My mind is full of cosmic images – strange stars, magical moons and distant planets, spinning in a dark sky.

Now I feel ready to explore my inner depths.

Back in normo-world Mum's pottering downstairs and I can hear Dad reading Max a bedtime story, so no one should disturb me.

It's time to become a Gothic Goddess.

Let the transformation begin!

Skyclad (except for a toga-style towel) I head to the bathroom, clutching everything I need. Carefully locking the door I turn on the taps and sprinkle lavender oil into the running water.

This is my ritual cleansing bath – to wash away the old, normo-Maddy. Then I mix up my black hair dye potion as instructed and load it onto a brush.

Finally I stand in front of the mirror and take one last look at the ginger curls framing my face...

Suddenly I freeze with fear.

What if the dye reacts badly?

What if my hair turns green??

Or purple??!!

Or falls out??!!!!

Maybe I should flush it down the pan and stay as I am...

GODDESS EXPRESS — YOUR QUICK GUIDE!

Think about your favourite goddess when you need her power.

Here are five fabulous names to get you started — Athene, Isis, Artemis, Venus, Morrigan...

No, I must be strong.

I must call on goddess-power.

I've read all about them and I choose Morrigan to help me now. She's a genuine Gothic Goddess — a warrior queen who rules Fate, Sorcery and Passionate Love.

She even takes the form of a raven sometimes – how Gothic is that?

Morrigan wouldn't be scared of a bowl of black hair dye!

Fate has handed me this chance to transform myself and I have to take it.

I grab a strand of hair and paint it black.

Very black.

Now there's no going back...

♡　★　♡

An hour later, I'm looking in my bedroom mirror at a mysterious stranger.

Her hair hangs in dark, wet snakes around her face. Her newly eye-lined eyes are deep pools of mystery and magic. No longer skyclad, she's wearing a silky wide-sleeved gown with a dragon motif on the back...

(Mad's note: I swapped my old, fluffy dressing gown for something more suitable from Mum's wardrobe.)

The girl staring back at me is ready for some serious spell-casting.

I lay out all the ingredients like before but don't want to repeat what Starr and I did earlier. This has to be an *Über-Strong Love Spell* that won't let me down.

Then I find a feature in *Lost Soul* about writing your own spell, which sounds perfect till I read it all:

DIY LOVE SPELLS

Making your own spells is a great way to express your creativity, but don't forget — even magic has its own rules!

The golden rule of Love Spells is that you must NOT use them to trap a certain someone by naming them.

WARNING

Do not call your love by name
Do not seek to make a claim
You must not force love with your spell
Remember this and all is well.

So, tell the universe you're ready for love...
Then wait to be sent the right person — whoever that might be!

The golden rule makes me *sooo* disappointed!

I don't want the universe to sort out my love life...it might send me any old sad-act-normo.

Now I've turned into a true Gothic Goddess and I feel like a total rebel.

Farewell dowdy daytime Maddy and welcome Madalena – cunning creature of the night!

Caspar LeStrange is the one for me and I don't think there's any harm in spelling it out. In fact, I think using his name in my spell will make it *über-powerful*!

It's time to reverse all the rules and make my own dark magic...

So now the candle is lit, the joss sticks are smoking and the new moon of love is beaming down through the gap in the curtains.

I sprinkle the rose-petals with oil, stirring them to release their sad, sweet scent and draw Caspar LeStrange to me.

Suddenly I'm chanting:

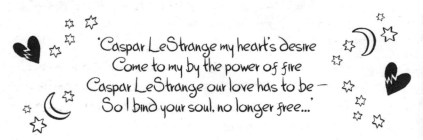

'Caspar LeStrange my heart's desire
Come to my by the power of fire
Caspar LeStrange our love has to be –
So I bind your soul, no longer free...'

I collect up all the rose petals and drop them into a little red velvet bag, tying it up tightly. Then I bind him with my words:

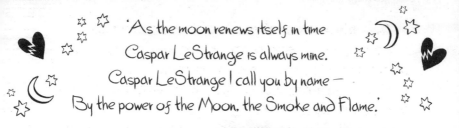

'As the moon renews itself in time
Caspar LeStrange is always mine.
Caspar LeStrange I call you by name –
By the power of the Moon, the Smoke and Flame.'

The candle flame flares up, spitting angrily like a warning. It reminds me that I must say the final two lines to seal the spell safely – even a Gothic Goddess wouldn't leave that bit out.

I pick up two joss sticks, wafting them around like wands when—

'AAAaaaagh!!!'

Something nips at my wrist like an evil imp and I look down to see my sleeve on fire.

'Help!!!!!! HELP!!!!!!!!!!!!!!!!!!!!'

As I dance around hysterically things get even worse. Suddenly a horrible noise starts up, shrieking like a wild witch at midnight – it's the smoke alarm!

Footsteps are drumming up the stairs, then there's shouting and banging and—

Crrrashhhhhh!!!!!!

Dad forces the door open and rushes in. He takes one look at me and throws the duvet over my shoulders, wrapping it around me and hugging me tight, putting out the flames in an instant.

Mum's right behind him. 'What's going on? Oh my goodness, what have you done to your beautiful hair?' she wails.

'Nothing – it'll wash out,' I babble.

She comes over as Dad rushes out muttering about the alarm, Max and the neighbours.

'I just lit a candle and...well...' I hold up the scorched sleeve. 'It isn't serious – it was a bit of a shock, that's all.'

'Candle?' Dad says sternly, walking back in. 'And what's that smell? Have you been smoking joss sticks?'

'Nooo! You don't smoke them – you light them to create a magical atmosphere—'

'Magic?' Mum looks at me in disbelief. 'I don't know what's got into you, Maddy! Taking my things, starting a fire and dabbling in magic? Whatever next?'

7

SPOT THE
GOTH

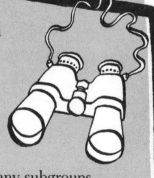

Romantigoth

Cybergoth Vampigoth

GOTH ROCK **Goth Punk**

Goth Metal

Mopey Goth **SARKY GOTH**

Perky Goth

The Goth movement spawns many subgroups…
So how can you spot the Goth?

'Maddy, what happened to your hair…and your eyes?'
Scott says when he calls round next morning. 'Are you
sick? You look like death warmed over.'

'Thanks, it's corpse-chic. I take that as a compliment.'
I flick back my newly straightened black hair and bat
my black-lined lashes. 'Should go down well at the
tryouts tonight.'

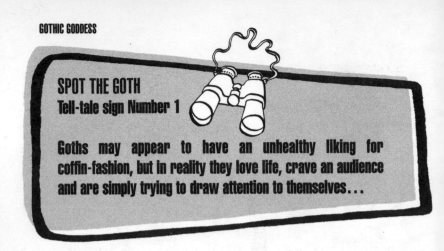

SPOT THE GOTH
Tell-tale sign Number 1

Goths may appear to have an unhealthy liking for
coffin-fashion, but in reality they love life, crave an audience
and are simply trying to draw attention to themselves...

'Oh yeah, the Gothic drama – might have guessed,' he
says as I close the front door and we set off for school. 'So
how did your folks take the fact that their sweet, red-
haired daughter was spirited away in the night and
replaced by a zom—'

'Gothic Goddess,' I interrupt. 'Oh, they're so normo –
there's no room in their life for Gothic Grandeur. I was
doing a little Gothic Magic last night and they got into a
total panic – I thought I'd never hear the end of it.'

'Why, what happened?'

'Nothing – just a little accident with a burning candle!
Anyway, I've agreed to do extra chores for the next two
weeks to make up for it. At least they didn't ground me –
I'd have missed the tryouts tonight and that would have
been tragic!'

'No it wouldn't. World poverty, climate change, animal
cruelty, now that's tragic! I see you're practising for the
melodrama already.'

'Yeah and it's going to be Gothically good tonight,

Scott. Why don't you skip the school council and come with us?'

I scrabble around in my pocket and pull out an eye-liner pencil. 'Here, this'll help you look the part,' I say, moving towards him.

'Back off, Maddy. I'm not into eye-liner!'

'Guy-liner,' I correct him. 'Very fashionable with emo lads these days.'

'Stop trying to label me!' Scott says. 'I'm not emo, normo, Gotho or anything else – just my own person.'

'OK, I get the point,' I say, poking his arm with the end of the pencil as a feeble joke.

I check out my new image in every shop window we pass on the way to school and feel pretty upbeat about it (if that's possible in Goth world) until we're almost there...

Then suddenly dark doubts descend out of nowhere and flit around my mind like blood-crazed bats.

What if people look at me and don't see a Gothic Goddess?

What if all they see is a Great Big Mess?

Now I want to turn around and run back to my lovely room. My cosy tomb of a room where I can stay sealed up and safe forever.

But it's too late.

The school day lies ahead of me – as inevitable as death, destiny and the drama tryouts at twilight.

♧　★　♡

'Omigoth, I'm so nervous I'm shaking,' I say to Starr. School's finished at last and we're making our way down the path to the Old Annexe.

'Don't be,' she says. 'Lots of people said they liked the new you, didn't they?'

'Yeah, more people spoke to me today than in the whole of my last year at school – including quite a few boys. It was *über-freaky*!'

'See – that should boost your confidence. At least you know you've done everything you can to look the part. So if you don't make it into the film then it wasn't meant to be.'

'Don't say that!' I panic. 'My whole life has been leading up to this point. I'm going to be Caspar's leading lady. It's written in the stars and sealed with a spell. If it doesn't happen then what's the point of *anything*?'

SPOT THE GOTH
Tell-tale sign Number 2

A true Goth milks the melodrama out of every mundane situation. Look for someone saying 'what's the point?' at least five times daily.

'Let's change the subject,' Starr says sensibly. 'Tell me about the Old Annexe. I've never been here before.'

We come to a door in the wall at the end of the

school grounds. I lift the latch and when we step through it's like walking into another world. The gravel path is quite overgrown, and dense evergreen trees block out the light, making it seem darker than it really is.

'It used to be a chapel years ago – now it's used for music and drama. They couldn't knock it down when the school was rebuilt because it's a listed building or something.'

Ahead of us is an old, ivy-clad stone building. The dark stained-glass windows are lit up and glow like old jewels in the gloom.

'It's fabulously Gothic,' I breathe.

'*Mmm* – wouldn't it be great to design some clothes inspired by this place?'

'And when you're rich and famous you can come back here for the fashion shoot!' I say.

'Yes, and see it on the front cover of *Vogue*,' Starr sighs. 'I *wish*...'

My heart thumps as we open the creaky wooden door and step inside. I can't believe I'm actually going to meet Caspar LeStrange again, after all these days of thinking about him.

We follow the *Lady and the Vamp* signs till we hear a voice coming from the room ahead. A voice that's deep and dramatic and stirs my soul with its wonderful words.

'...More of a mix of *Romeo and Juliet* meets *Dracula*,' it's saying. 'I keep some of Shakespeare's better ideas – the tombs, the tragedy and the tortured love, but twist them like a sadist's slipknot...'

We're almost at the door now and I can see a group of Gothic-looking types sitting on chairs while a tall, black-clad figure (with even taller, messed-up hair) is speaking to them.

Even though he's got his back to us, I'd know him anywhere.

'That's *him*,' I hiss at Starr, as we stand in the doorway. 'The Gorgeous Goth.'

'It's OK. You can go in and sit down,' says the nearest Goth, who comes over. He's round and jolly and a bit too smiley to carry off the true Goth look. 'Caspar's just setting the scene.'

He waves us to some seats and Caspar LeStrange pauses mid-breath as we walk into the room.

'Welcome to the Dark Side!' he says as we move along the row.

At the sound of his voice my face fires up instantly.

Nooo!

Whoever heard of a blotchy-red Goth?

Starr sits down looking pale, pallid and interesting, while I can feel a prickly red rash creeping up my neck. *Why Me???*

(*Mad's note: Not so much Spot the Goth as Spotty Goth.*)

I sit down and keep my eyes on the floor in embarrassment as Caspar continues. 'You're just in time to hear the background to my Gothic drama. Like I said, it's based on Shakespeare's star-crossed lovers, but what actually divides them?'

Now I'm bursting to speak. This is so spooky – we're doing *Romeo and Juliet* in English right now and it's my all-time favourite play! Of course, he probably doesn't want an answer – he's just pausing for dramatic effect.

Say nothing, I think. *Don't draw attention to yourself. Keep cool and wait for the blotches to blend in. That's what's best.*

But before I know it someone's speaking – and it's me!

'Romeo and Juliet can't be together because of a family bust-up way back,' I say. 'Shakespeare calls it an *ancient grudge—*'

Then I stop.

Everyone's looking at me and I know I must sound like such a nerdy know-all.

Nooo!

I want to curl up and die – until Caspar strides over in two steps and towers over me with a gleam in his eye.

'Impressive!' he says, looking amused. 'Have we met before?' he gives a mock bow and takes my hand. 'I'm Caspar LeStrange. And you are…?'

SPOT THE GOTH
Tell-tale sign Number Three

Goths change their name to fit their image.
Look for names of obscure European nobility with nocturnal overtones.

Note: If you meet someone with a name like Caspar Nightmare, Vladimir Bloodcrave or Vampira Darkshadow – chances are they're a Goth.

'I'm Mad...' I squeak, as my nerve fails me. Someone sniggers.

'Ah, we all are – that's the irony of life,' he says. 'It's just that most people don't admit it.'

'I mean I...I'm Madalena,' I mutter. 'Madalena Velvetcrush.'

'Maddy?!' Starr's looking at me as if I really am mad. 'What are you talking about?'

Caspar hears her but we're in Goth-world now and he understands.

'Madalena Velvetcrush – I'm charmed,' he says, bowing his head. 'A dark-haired girl with a brain and a wondrous name. I won't forget.'

He walks back to the front and it goes quiet. 'As we've just heard, Romeo and Juliet were divided by a family argument but I've Gothed it up a bit for my film.'

He starts to pace around restlessly and his hair stands on end as if lightning is sparking out of his brain.

'So, what if Romeo was a vampire?' He throws his arms open in a dramatic gesture. 'What if he falls for a mortal girl – a normo – and she loves him too?'

Caspar stalks over and stands in front of us, lowering his voice so we have to strain to hear him as he whispers, 'What if they're desperate for a kiss? Just one kiss – a harmless kiss to express their burning love for each other. Therein lies the tragedy.'

He pauses again and my lips are dry with the thought of that desperate kiss.

'For if they kiss – Juliet is condemned to the same living

hell that Romeo suffers. She will be turned into a vampire, destined to feast on human blood for the rest of her...living death.'

Caspar looks round at us all. 'Romeo doesn't want to do that, does he? Transform his girlfriend into one of the Undead. Oh, but how can they resist one kiss? One fangtastic kiss?'

And as he says that I swear he's looking straight at me...

8

MOJO
BAGS

Mojo bags

Did you know you can carry a spell round with you?

For extra power, keep your spell in a mojo – a little drawstring bag – and carry it with you in a secret place.

We recommend love spells are worn close to the heart at all times.

Spoooky!

I seem to have scored a hit with Caspar and it's all because of my mojo!

It's hidden inside my jacket pocket close to my beating heart – as recommended by *Lost Soul's* Top Ten Spelling Tips. This bag of DIY magic is binding Caspar to me!

'So there you have it – that's the story of *Lady and the Vamp*. It's a terrible tragedy... Normo Juliet Mortal meets vampire Romeo Diabolo, played by yours truly.' Caspar gives a little bow, winks and then disappears out of the door, his cloak swirling around him like a dark mist.

Omigoth! He's overloading my psychic switchboard with secret messages. It doesn't take a clairvoyant to predict the future (well the next few hours, at least).

Caspar's going to cast me in the lead as Juliet and the rest is obvious – it's a well-known fact that actors always fall for their leading ladies.

I'm *sooo* glad I Gothed-up like all the others here. Black hair, eyes, lips and nails.

Poor Starr stands out a bit with her blonde hair and barely-there make-up. I hope she doesn't feel too left out – but I suppose what she looks like doesn't really matter as she only came along to give me moral support.

'Don't you just love the way Caspar improved on Shakespeare and changed Romeo and Juliet's last names? *Mortal and Diabolo* – he's a Goth Genius!' I say when he's gone.

'Hmm, he's not really my type. Bit too over-the-top – I get enough drama at home.'

'So you don't think he's Goth-tastic?'

Starr shakes her head, 'Nope, can't see it, I'm afraid.'

Now I don't know whether to be:

a. Insulted that she doesn't like my taste in boys
b. Relieved that Starr with her supermodel looks isn't any kind of rival

She must have seen the look on my face because she adds, 'Oh...but he seemed to like you. He's a few years older than us though, isn't he?'

'Age is just a number,' I say, 'Especially if you're a vampire.'

'Then you're a match made in heaven,' she laughs.

'Heaven?' I raise a Gothic eyebrow.

'Er...hell,' she corrects herself.

'That's better – ten points on the Goth-o-meter! It's a new way of looking at things – just embrace your dark side. Remember the rules – *Good=Bad, Gloom=Glad.* It's easy—'

'Greetings everyone!'

The Smiley Goth stands up now and starts speaking. 'We're going to see you all one at a time. When your name's called you'll have a few minutes to get changed before the tryout. We've got some costumes in the prop-room to help you get in role. It's over there.'

He points out of the door and across the corridor. 'The room leads on to the back of the stage and that's where you'll act your scene. Good luck!'

'Will you be able to stay?' I ask Starr, knowing that she's worried about her dad. He's quite capable of being lost in his music and forgetting to open the bar.

'Yes, it's OK. Matt's taken on a relief manager and she's very organised. I warned him I'd be late. He told me to take all the time I needed.'

'Good, that's—'

'Hi, it's Maddy, isn't it?' the Smiley Goth interrupts, looking at me. 'I didn't recognise you at first.

Normally you stand out from the crowd with your lovely red hair...'

I give him my blackest, Gothic scowl.

'Oh, er...not that I don't like your hair now,' he backtracks. 'It's...er...*different*. Well no...actually it's the same as all the rest. Oh, I didn't mean...' He stops and shrugs. 'Sorry, I've got a bit of a thing about redheads.'

He's still smiling but I'm not happy – who does he think he is, giving out free hair-care hints?

I decide to give it to him straight. 'A) My name's not Maddy, it's *Madalena*, and B) I'm no longer a redhead, I'm a *blackhead*.'

Then I give him the evil eye but he doesn't take the hint. He just laughs and says, 'Nice one,' and looks all twinkly and eager.

Weird!

'Excuse me, but do we actually know each other?' I ask, wondering which extra-large coffin he's crawled out of.

'Oh, well, sort of... We're in the same year at school but you probably never noticed me. I've seen you, though – you were on stage, weren't you? The Head said it was your idea to have that fashion show to raise money for the children's hospital. That was a masterstroke!'

I try not to smile, but my lips might have twitched slightly. 'And your name is...?'

'Nathaniel...Nat. Everyone calls me Fat Nat.' He shrugs his shoulders and laughs good-naturedly.

'Nat, you're on,' Caspar calls.

Über-swoon – just hearing his velvety voice makes my

stomach flutter like a startled bat.

'That's me,' Nat smiles. 'Or rather, my alter ego' – he puts on a deep, evil voice like a horror movie voiceover – *'Nocturnus Mortal – Juliet's fiery cousin. Mwa-ha-haa.'*

'Bye then,' I say, hoping we can get on with it.

'Good luck with the audition!' Nat gives me a little wave with his stubby fingers. *'That's all folks, exit stage left!'* he squeaks cartoon-style as he finally leaves.

When he's gone, Starr looks at me with interest. 'That love spell you cast,' she says. 'I thought you said it didn't work?'

'Well it didn't! So I made up my own spell and performed it later.' Suddenly an image of me chanting Caspar's name by candlelight flashes into my head.

'It was an *Über-Strong Love Spell,*' I add, smiling.

'I'll say,' she agrees. 'Must have been at least double strength!'

9

GOOD LUCK
CHARMS

Good luck symbols and charms are used to attract positive energy.

Choose from the list below to find the best one to help you!

Flower = inspiration charm
Key = empowerment charm
Clover = luck charm
Heart = love and friendship charm

Waiting for the tryout is like sitting in some kind of Gloomy Gothic Dentist's Waiting Room.

It's dark outside and the wind is whistling through the windows. Inside candles are flickering, casting weird shadows on the walls.

Every time a name is called out a shiver of whispers runs through the group. Then someone disappears to the prop room, never to return...

Finally only Starr and I are left. We huddle together and I'm starting to feel totally creeped out.

At last Nat, the smiley Goth, comes in. 'Sorry it's taking so long,' he says. 'We're having a quick break and we'll see you both in turn.' He winks. 'We saved you both till last because we've got a couple of key parts we thought you'd be good for.'

My heart suddenly stops. Caspar must have told him he's saved the part of Juliet for me! I feel like my future happiness is already written down in the book of Fate – now all I have to do is turn the page.

'Madalena!'

I grip Starr's arm tightly. Hearing Caspar's voice leaves me paralysed with fear. What if I mess up?

'Can't move,' I say through gritted teeth. 'Think I've got rigor mortis.'

Starr feels my wrist. 'No, there's still a pulse. Go on – this is the moment you've been waiting for!' She peels my hand away. 'Just be yourself. Knock 'em dead!'

'The prop room's over there.' Nat stands at the door waving me over. I stagger to my feet and follow his directions.

'Good luck!' he says and disappears.

Fate has brought me to this point and I should trust it for the next few minutes, but I can't. That's why I need to keep my mojo bag close by. Not only are the actual rose petals from my love spell inside it, but I've added some good luck charms for extra power.

Did you know?

In the old days, good luck charms could be anything from roots and herbs to rattlesnake rattles, dried frogs and bat wings.

(Modern urban girls prefer to use lucky paper charms, toys or tokens.)

Due to a lack of rattlesnakes and bat wings, I used confetti left over from when we went to a wedding last year. The shapes are just right – flowers, hearts, keys and four-leaved clovers – a great mix to keep me covered for all occasions.

I root through a pile of clothes on the table, all in various shades of black, and hold them up to the mirror. Yes, Lady Luck is smiling on me... It looks like Goth clothes can be quite flattering to the, er, fuller figure, like mine.

There's a long, scoop-necked dress, which has a high waist and is laced up at the front, and it looks perfect. When I put it on it hides all my worst bits – the lumps, bumps and thunder thighs.

Now the Glamorous Gothic Goddess Lady Madalena is staring back at me through her poker-straight curtains of hair. Is that really me, I wonder?

I touch up the eye-liner and black lipstick, but even Gothed-up, I'm still feeing jittery and superstitious.

The problem is – where to hide my mojo?

It must be worn close to the heart, but how? I'm not wearing my jacket so it'll have to go inside my dress. The scoop neckline is a lot lower than I'd normally wear.

(Mad's note: Luckily it looks more vampy than trampy.)

But when I tuck the mojo down the front it looks plain *freaky*. Three bumps – that won't work. Not unless there's some mythical three-breasted goddess I haven't heard about.

'Everything OK in there?' Nat's knocking at the door now.

'Yes, just coming!' I call.

Now I'm panicking.

Desperate times call for desperate measures.

I open up the drawstring bag and pour the contents down the front of my dress. Luckily the broad band of elastic around the high waistline keeps the confetti and rose petals safely in place. Then I joggle myself around a bit till everything's nestling naturally.

I smile at my reflection. All that padding's given me a cleavage – I've never had one of those before! Then I pout – remembering that Gothic Goddesses don't grin – and sweep out onto the stage.

Caspar's standing there, looking tall and Goth-gorgeous in a black ruffled shirt, open at the throat, and a long velvet cape fastened at his neck with a silver clasp.

'Lady Madalena, how charming. He gives me a mock bow. Then he takes a deep breath, strikes a pose and launches straight into the script.

'Scene two – the Masked Ball. You are Juliet Mortal and

you've just met me, Romeo Diabolo. We fall instantly in love.'

I give a nervous laugh and turn it into a cough. Gothic Goddesses don't giggle, either.

'We are just about to kiss—' he leans towards me and I close my eyes. I can feel his warm breath on my cheek as he murmurs, '*Mmm*, what's that perfume you're wearing? It smells of lost love and faded summers…'

I open my eyes to find him looking right at me, or rather my chest. My body heat must have activated the scent of the lavender oil and rose petals.

'Oh, it's exclusive, I mixed it myself. It's called um…*Romantic Decay*.'

'Fascinating.' He looks into my eyes. 'Captivating,' he adds, and now I don't know if he's acting or not.

The moment is dripping with destiny. I'm sure the spell is working and he's falling in love with me.

He moves even closer, breathing in the scent of my magical, mystical mojo.

I close my eyes and pucker up…

'*STOP!*'

A loud voice booms out, breaking the spell. My eyes snap open to see Nat charging towards us.

> '*Stop, you fiend! Leave my cousin alone!*
> *Withdraw your fangs and fly away home —*
> *Back to your coffin, somewhere cold and damp.*
> *You're not a guest, you're a bloodthirsty Vamp!*'

Nat's at Caspar's throat now, almost strangling him.

'*Gerroff!*' I shriek, whacking him on the arm. 'Leave him alone!'

He lets go of Caspar, who swirls his velvet cape and wheels offstage.

Swwwwwwwoooooosh!

Nat clasps my shoulders and looks steadily at me. 'Great acting – you're really convincing. Now read this, it's your solo scene.'

Then he runs off shouting, '*I'll get you, Romeo Diabolo! Aaaaaaggggggrrrrrr!*'

Suddenly I'm left alone in the spotlight, my mind whirling. It's hard to tell drama from real life at this point.

When I stare down at the words written on the page they could have been ripped from my own heart. I take a deep breath, throwing myself into the role, pacing the floor, gesturing wildly...

'Torn apart – and no passionate kiss!
Torn apart – and no moment of bliss!'

Then I sink down and slump forward dramatically, whispering the next heartrending words:

'Can it be true, the words my cousin spoke?
Romeo's a vampire, is this some kind of joke?'

Now I jump up, tearing my hair and beating my chest for maximum impact...

> *'O woe is me! Before we can be wed,*
> *He must drink my blood to make me Undead!*
> *So that's my choice...to be Romeo's wife –*
> *I must give up my body (thump) my soul (thump)...my life!'*

I give a final thump of my chest and bow my head. That's when I see that I've been losing leaves like a tree in a storm and I'm standing in a puddle of confetti and rose petals.

No! Spooktacular cringe!

All that chest-beating sent clouds of *Lucky-Lurve-Litter* fluttering out with every dramatic gesture.

How do I explain that away?

Caspar will think I've tried to impress him with home-made, home-grown breast implants or something and I can hardly tell him the truth about my magical mojo...

Suddenly I hear clapping and the two boys are on the stage.

'Cool special effects!' Nat's saying.

'Love the dried roses,' Caspar agrees. 'Symbolic of your love for Romeo, which dried and withered on the stem before it could bloom?'

I nod energetically, 'S...symbolic? Yes, that's it – of course.'

'And the confetti?'

'Represents the wedding they may never have,' I say

quickly, blowing away a stray pink heart which has landed on my nose.

(Mad's note: Desperation is the mother of inspiration in Mad-world.)

'Such passion – you were very convincing, Madalena Velvetcrush.' Caspar clasps my hand theatrically and kisses it.

I'm in heaven...sorry, Gothic heaven, which is hell, of course.

'You'd be perfect as...'

He pauses but I don't mind the dramatic tease. He's obviously blown away by my performance and is definitely going to cast me as—

'Hysterica Diabolo. You have all the right qualities. Doesn't she, Nat?'

'Hysterica? Who...?'

'My mother and Vampiress-in-Chief. It's a wonderful part. She's a complete drama-diva and—'

'Your *mother*?' Did I hear him right? 'Not... um...Juliet?' I say, trying to hide my disappointment. Hysterica doesn't sound like me at all.

'Well, no. I'm afraid you wouldn't be right for Juliet. She isn't a vamp, of course – that's the whole point. She's a normo, so we need a non-Goth for that role. Your friend out there – the natural-looking one with the blonde hair. She looks perfect for the part.'

He smiles and flashes his brilliant white teeth. 'We'll give her a black wig when she's corrupted by me. As long as she can string a few words together, she'll do.'

'Congratulations,' Nat says, grabbing my hand and shaking it. 'You've got a character role, just like me.'

'Character role?' I repeat, stupidly.

'Yes, and the good thing is we got our parts because of our acting skills – *not* our looks!'

After all the trouble I took to Goth-up – the hair, the eyes, the nails – I'm even wearing black underwear!

All that trouble and Caspar wanted a normo, not a Goth! Oh, the tragic irony of life…

Nat shrugs and smiles. 'Juliet's really quite bland and boring. Hysterica's more of a challenge, isn't she?'

He's digging a hole here – like a gravedigger on a deadline – but he doesn't seem to notice.

'I mean, who wants the lead role anyway?' he adds cheerfully.

I stare at him in a state of speechless Gothic gloom.

10

MAGICAL
ANIMALS

**We can have one or more
animals as spirit guides. These are
the so-called power animals. They
are always there to help us and
normally invisible in the 'real world'.**

Which animal is yours?

'So did the magical, mystical spell work?' Scott asks next
morning when he calls for me. Did you get the star part?'

'Yee...es,' I say, not looking him in the eye. 'I got a part,
thank you. I'm Hysterica Diabolo. Not the lead but it's a
very demanding role. I'm very lucky. Lots of girls would
die for the chance to play it.' I hitch my backpack over my
shoulder and set off down the road.

I don't want him to see how upset I am. Last night
I could hardly sleep. I was sure the love spell had worked,
so what went wrong? Why didn't I get Juliet?

Then I woke up this morning, scanned my mag and felt
a bit better. Maybe the universe is moving in a mysterious

way. After all, the fact that I'm not playing Juliet doesn't stop Caspar and I getting together.

According to *Lost Soul* you have to wait for Fate to give you a few clues and show you the way on your true life-path. It lists a good website on spirit guides and magical animals I thought I'd check out later...

'So who got the leading role?' Scott says, catching me up.

'Starr, she's playing Juliet,' I say, trying to sound casual.

'But I thought she wanted to do costume design,' Scott says, mystified. 'I didn't think she wanted to act.'

'Well no, but I persuaded her that Destiny had decreed it, so she should have a go. Even then she was worried about how I'd feel.'

'Yeah – me too. Next thing we know you'll steal her nail clippings and make a little voodoo wax Starr-doll to stick pins in...'

'Scott – I'm over all that *jealousy junkie** stuff! I'm cool with Starr acting opposite Caspar.'

'Very noble, Maddy, impressive.'

'Anyway if she'd refused to do it, Goth knows who he might have picked! At least I know Starr doesn't fancy him,' I sigh.

'Oh, I get it – better the devil you know,' Scott laughs. 'Not so noble but much more believable.'

'That's so unfair! Starr's perfect for the role and she asked Caspar if I could be her understudy, just in case anything happens. You know how things are for her at home...'

*Read *Jealousy Junkie* by Carrie Bright to find out about Scott's first meeting with Starr and why Maddy fell out with Scott!

He nods. 'Yeah, at least the acting will keep her busy. Oh and can you both meet me at lunchtime in the Resource Centre? The school council wants a brilliant new idea to raise cash for a good cause and as you did so well last time...'

We're nearly at school now and Starr's waiting for us at the gates.

'Scott needs our brainpower at lunch,' I tell her. 'Earth-shattering ideas for fundraising – again!'

♥ ★ ♡

Three hours later we're sitting in the Resource Centre trying to come up with an original idea. Scott told us to check the school website to find out what's been done in the last five years.

'Of course, we wouldn't have this problem if you hadn't been voted onto the school council,' I say.

'Can't help it, just call me Mr Popular,' Scott says modestly, tapping at the keyboard.

'No...you're a bee. A definite bee, wouldn't you say, Starr?' I add, pointing at the screen we're sharing.

'Watcha on about girl – are you disrespecting me?' Scott puts on his street voice. 'I ain't no B...!'

Starr's laughing. 'Maddy's looking at alternative websites,' she says.

'Yeah, you should take a look, Scott. It was recommended in *Lost Soul*.' I flap my mag at him. 'You can find out all about your Magical Animal and call on it in times of need!'

'*These are the bee's magical qualities*,' Starr reads aloud...

BEE

One who has the power of the Bee will be focussed and hardworking. The Bee shows us how to co-operate with others to achieve ultimate success for the good of the community.

bzzzzzz

'*Tcha!*' Scott sucks his teeth in disgust.

'It's you!' I say. 'Working hard all the time for others.' I wag my finger at him. 'But don't forget to take time out to smell the flowers. Bees have to do that, too.'

'Not in here they don't,' he says. 'I thought you two were going to help me, not waste time on the world-wide-weirdy-web.'

'Oh, look – dolphins – they're my favourite!' Starr says, scrolling down the magical animals pages.

'Let's see what their qualities are, then.' I focus on the screen.

DOLPHIN

The beautiful, graceful and sleek Dolphin tells us how to move with the ebb and flow of life instead of fighting the current and getting nowhere. Dolphins show us joy and harmony in all things.

'*Spooky!* – now do you believe me, Scott? Beautiful, graceful, moves well. That is so like Starr!' I turn to her. 'And harmony must mean your talent for fashion design and the way you can pick out colours that go together. Maybe you were a dolphin in a former life—'

'And maybe you were an annoying little dung beetle in a former life,' Scott interrupts, glaring at me. 'Oh, my mistake, that's what you are now.'

'See – that's your sting. Very sharp, too,' I say. 'A definite bee – or maybe a wasp.'

'Maddy, this is important – school council's depending on me! I'm supposed to come up with a plan but it's all been done before. What are we going to raise money for? How are we going to do it? Now focus!'

I try to, I really do, but it's very hard not to get distracted. Starr joins Scott at his computer and makes a few suggestions, but when Scott looks into them it's obvious this isn't going to be easy.

'Fun run?'

'Er...done two years ago.'

'Sponsored silence?'

'Zzzzzzzzz. Bor-ring.'

Meanwhile I start matching up people I know with their Magical Animal. Maybe it'll help me understand how to handle them better.

Caspar's first. I look up 'bat' but it's not quite him so I try 'owl' and it's perfect.

OWL: creature of the night

The Owl is a shape shifter,
using the moon's power to
explore the inner world
of secrets and shadows. It
has the courage to follow
its instincts.

Yes, that definitely sounds like a Gothic writer and would-be vampire. He's a creature of the night – and I hope his instincts will lead him straight to me.

Now, what about my animal? In my new Gothic phase I can see myself as a mysterious black cat...

'Cats!'

I stare at the screen mesmerised for a moment.

'Cats!' I repeat. 'That's our answer! Look, Scott – cats!'

'Maddy, this isn't funny any more. Shut up about those Magical Animals, will you!'

Scott sounds angry, but he's got it all wrong.

'No, Scott. I've had a vision. It's seeing the cat picture that did it. I must be psychic. I've been on a magical *Tour de Trance* and it took me to the future. The fundraising – I saw everything!'

'Everything?'

'Yes! I know the charity we can raise money for and I know exactly how to do it. Trust me. I have the power...'

11

CAT-POWER

CAT

If the cat is your power animal, then you have magic and mystery in your life.
You are independent, curious, unpredictable and free-thinking.

Cats also represent love...

'Look,' I say, pulling my purse out of my bag and producing something that came with my Mystic Market goodies.

Scott and Starr stare blankly at the white card between my fingers.

So I turn it over and point to the back:

RAVEN'S CAT RESCUE CENTRE

We rescue, foster and relocate all cats – especially black cats.

The Cat Rescue Centre is an independent charity.
Please give generously – and save a cat today!

Scott takes the card and examines it carefully. 'Hmm, it's very local and the school hasn't supported an animal charity before, but how can we help?'

'*Goth-up and cough up!*' I say. 'Everyone pays to come to school Gothed-up, so they get a non-uniform day and we raise plenty of money.'

'O...*kay*,' Scott says. 'So why would they want to do that? What's the hook?'

'Saving cats, of course – and everyone loves a day to dress up! Plus the best-dressed Goths win tickets to the glamorous Goth Film Gala Night after school.'

'What glamorous Goth Film Gala Night?' Scott looks confused.

'The first showing of *Lady and the Vamp* – Caspar's original, award-winning film.'

'But it hasn't won any awards!' Scott's still not following.

'Then we'll have to make some up and award them on the night. It's got to be over-the-top Goth!'

'We could have the actors making an entrance on a long, red carpet,' Starr says, getting into the spirit of things. 'Decorate the hall with mirrors, white lilies, candles, cobwebs and crushed-velvet cushions.'

'OK, OK it's got potential, but we need to talk to a few people about it first.'

'Like—?'

'Like this Raven, whoever she is!' Scott says. 'Find out more about the cat rescue project.'

'Oh, that's easy – she runs the Mystic Market stall, remember?'

'And Caspar. We need to talk to him, too. Didn't you tell me he's making this film for his Performing Arts project? How do you know he'll want to be involved?'

'Oh, I think he will,' I say, confidently. 'You can't fight Fate, and look how everything came together just like that!' I click my fingers like a magician performing a spell. 'Call me a silly psychic but something tells me this is meant to happen.'

Scott still isn't totally sold on the idea, but luckily, when he wants something done, he moves *fast*!

By the end of the school day he's fixed up for us to meet Caspar at Raven's house after school.

Now, sitting on the bus, I'm tingling with excitement. *Weird!*

My super-psychic powers are sending me flashes from the future and I've got plenty to smile about.

(Mad's note: I'm smiling on the inside, of course, but on the outside I remain Gothically grim.)

In my vision I can see Caspar, thanking me for the whole *Goth-up and Cough-up* project...

Not only that, but I can see a glamorous Goth couple leading the way down the red carpet into school... OK, I can't see their faces but my sixth sense tells me it's Lady Madalena Velvetcrush and Caspar LeStrange – the leading couple in Gothic gorgeosity!

Yes, this Goth Film Gala Night is going to bring us together. Don't ask me how I know – I just do!

(Mad's note: Psychic powers improve with use. It's like your mind is a mental pencil sharpener.)

♥ ⭐ ♡

'This is it,' Scott says, standing at the gate of a fairly normal-looking house.

At least, the house appears that way on the surface...

Of course, now that I'm a Gothic Goddess, I can spot the little clues that point to its shadow life.

a. There's a sticker in the front window with a black cat silhouette on it. (Black cat = magic)
b. Wind chimes tinkle eerily on the breeze. (Wind chimes = ward off evil spirits)
c. There's a lot of ivy, weird statues and a moss-covered fountain. (Gothic garden = spooky!)

'Can you see Caspar?' I ask hopefully. 'D'you think he's gone in already?'

'Hang on,' says Starr, 'is that him coming round the corner now?'

A dark shape appears, getting bigger, rounder, wavier and smilier at it draws near.

Definitely not Caspar LeStrange, Über-Prince of Darkness, but only Fat Nat – smiley Goth and Caspar's sidekick.

'Greetings!' he says, when he reaches us. 'I (puff) ran (phew) all the way. Hope (wheeze) you haven't (whoo!) been waiting long?'

'Where's Caspar?' I blurt out anxiously.

Scott shoots me a look. 'Thanks for coming, Nat,' he says. 'Take a minute to get your breath back and we'll go in. We've got time – it's only just six now.'

'Right...' Nat sits on the wall. 'Sorry, you've only got me, I'm afraid. Caspar sends his apologies. He forgot he had to pick up some props for tomorrow.'

'Rats...! I mean bats!' I can't hide my disappointment and plonk myself down on the wall next to him.

'He might come along later,' Nat says.

'Really?' I brighten up and look at him. 'Did he say he would?'

'*Mmm*, possibly,' Nat frowns. 'He's so busy on the creative side of things that he's leaving this charity stuff to me. He doesn't want to be distracted from his artistic mission...'

'But when I spoke to you earlier you said he'd be all for it.' Scott says looking puzzled.

'Yeah, don't get me wrong,' Nat gives one of his shrugs. 'I told him the film premiere would get us lots of free publicity, which he liked. It's just that his head is full of vampires and darkness and stuff – not a lot of room for cat charities.'

Suddenly the door opens and Raven jangles at us with her silvery bracelets. 'Hi! D'you want to come in, or are you waiting for someone?'

Omigoth – she's a real Glam-Goth with her dark velvet dress and shiny black hair! I want to be like that when I've moved from being a Gothling to a full-grown Goth.

Although, seeing her as a 'real person' and not behind a market stall, it strikes me that she only looks a year or two older than us. I'd like to interview her mag-style to find out more...

This week Madalena Velvetcrush has another in-depth interview. She asks Raven those all-important questions like:

a. **What's the story behind the stall and the cats?**
b. **How do you look so genuinely Gothic?**
c. **Were you *born* in crushed velvet?**

Scott moves towards the door and the others follow, but I want to wait here. I'm sure Caspar's going to turn up – and my sixth sense hasn't been wrong yet.

'Coming?' Starr says, holding the door open. The others have all gone in and my psychic powers are fading as fast as my feet are freezing.

There's still no sign of the Dark Prince of Gothitude.

Maybe I was wrong and Caspar's too busy to hear about my brilliant ideas?

I give in and walk up the drive with a heavy heart...

12

DREAM CATCHER

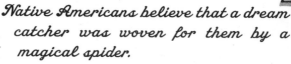

Native Americans believe that a dream catcher was woven for them by a magical spider.
The web was spun on a willow hoop, which had feathers, beads and offerings on it...

'*Omigoth!* Your house is amazing,' I say to Raven, looking round at the crystals, candles, new-agey trinkets and Gothic bric-a-brac which fill every available space.

'Yes, Mum is very alternative but she also works as an accountant to bring in some cash. She says there's no money in predicting the future but it's a big help when you're investing in stocks and shares,' Raven smiles.

'Do you mind me asking what these are?' Scott points at some feathery mobiles hanging down from the ceiling.

'Dream catchers,' I say. 'I read about them in *Lost Soul.*'

'That's right – they're my dad's. He's a traditional craftsman and makes anything from dream catchers to yurts.'

(Mad's note: Yurt? What's that - a yoghurt-flavoured tent?)

'And so many lovely cats!' Starr scoops one up from a chair and sits down with it in her lap. 'What—'

BBBBBBbbbring!

The doorbell interrupts and sets my spine tingling. The air is charged with electricity and it's Caspar, I just know it.

'I'll go!' I leap up and rush down the hall, opening the door to see him standing there in a Victorian top hat and tailcoat. *Sigh*, he's taller and more Gothic than ever.

'Ah, Lady Madalena!' He sweeps off his hat and gives a little bow.

I try to get into the spirit of things by attempting a little curtsey but end up tripping over the doormat and lunging at him.

'Oh, er...excuse me.' I put out my hands to stop myself falling and grab his hat, trying to make it look as if I did it on purpose.

'Let me take that,' I say, waving it around. 'Everyone's in there.'

'Thank you.' He hands me a silver-topped cane and strides through to the front room.

I pause to savour the moment.

The Prince of Darkness has just walked past me and I'm holding his *actual Gothic accessories*! I stroke his silky hat and silvery cane lovingly before putting them down and going in after him.

'Apologies for my tardiness,' Caspar's saying. 'I was unavoidably delayed with film-making and funerals.' He smiles mysteriously. 'Now what's all this Nat was telling me about cats?'

'It was an idea Maddy had to raise money for a good cause,' Starr says loyally. I know she's trying to make me look good in front of Caspar.

'Highly commendable, but I don't quite see how that fits in with *Lady and the Vamp*?' Caspar looks mystified. 'I mean – if we were performing *Cats, the Musical* it would make perfect sense, but what have cats got to do with a Gothic melodrama?'

Everyone looks a bit uncomfortable and I must admit, when he puts it like that even I have to agree with him. What was I thinking...? But my psychic vision was so vivid. I could see it all – the cats, the film gala, the Gorgeous Goth couple (a.k.a. you-know-who)...

Just then a black cat nuzzles up to Caspar and starts miaowing.

'That's Midnight,' Raven says. 'He was my first cat – he's the granddaddy of all the cats now. We think he's almost seventeen, the same age as me.'

Midnight's winding around Caspar's legs and he bends down to stroke him. 'Respect to Midnight,' he says. 'That's a name to conjure with.'

'He was my first rescue cat,' Raven says. 'We found him abandoned in a cardboard box in the park and he was in a bad way – hungry and dehydrated. I begged my parents to let me keep him. Luckily he survived but it was touch and go at one point... Not long after that Dad got into making dream catchers.' She gestures to the ones hanging in the room.

Dream catcher

The web is a perfect circle but there is a hole in the centre. If you are a believer it will sift your dreams, sending the bad ones through the holes and catching the good ones.

A dream catcher will help you make use of your ideas, dreams and visions...

'For years my dreams were filled with cats and more cats – especially black ones. When I left school last year I took time out to start Raven's Cat Rescue Centre – I want to get it established before going back to college.'

This is so inspiring. Even if Caspar wasn't involved, the more I hear about Raven's project the more I hope we can help her.

'So how many cats have you got? Where do they come from and what happens if...'

(I want to ask *if no new home is found for them* but I stop – maybe it's the Goth in me that's bringing out the gloomy questions.)

Raven guesses what I'm going to say. 'We are supposed to take them to be reassessed after three months, but as far as I can I operate a pro-life policy. Usually they end up living with us. We keep all the rejects.'

'Is this one you decided to keep?' Nat asks and I notice that he's playing with another black cat that has crept in.

This poor thing seems to have no tail...

'Yeah, that's Cobweb – she was brought to us after a traffic accident and no one stepped forward to claim her,' Raven says.

'Oh, who could resist claiming you?' Nat asks as Cobweb chases a piece of string she's found.

'Black cats are the most likely to be abandoned and least likely to be re-homed after rescue,' Raven says. 'When I found out, I decided to specialise in re-homing black cats. I believe that's what the dream catcher had been trying to show me.'

'As the only black person in the room, I'd like to ask why this black cat prejudice?' Scott says in mock protest. 'It's madness!'

'Crazy isn't it? I prefer black cats,' Raven says.

'Black cats are far more elegant,' Caspar agrees.

'I love them – I AM a black cat,' I say, determined not to be left out.

There's a stunned silence until Starr adds, 'She means it's her Magical Animal.'

Luckily Raven understands. 'Oh, I see. Yes, that's why I'm called Raven – my father worked out it was my Magical Animal when I was born.'

'You mean your real name is Raven – it's not...made up?' I say in awe.

'Yes, it's my real name. Oh, and I was born with a shock of black hair, which clinched it.'

(Mad's note: Raven's a true Goth through and through – no false names and black hair dye. Bow down and worship, all you wannabes!)

'Anyway, to answer your question, we have about ten cats in the pens outside and six in here. We have all sorts of cats but the black ones are usually left behind. I suppose some people see a black cat and think of bad luck.'

'Depressing,' Scott says.

'But they can mean the opposite too,' I say, reaching into my bag and flapping my mag around. I find the page on 'Feline Folklore' and read, *'Many people think that if a black cat crosses your path it brings good luck.'*

'That sounds better. Thanks for that, I take back everything I ever said about your trashy mags,' Scott smiles.

'Fascinating,' Caspar says to Midnight, who is now purring and staring into space with glazed, golden eyes. 'See? Not only are you stylishly dressed in fabulous black fur but you are also shunned and completely misunderstood. Truly, black cats are the Goths of the feline world!'

And as soon as Caspar says that I know the path of true love is running smoothly again.

He's been won over to the fundraising
and it was all my idea!
My date with Fate is drawing near.

We're destined to be together – as sure as my name is Madalena Velvetcrush, Mistress of the Dark Arts!

13

DEALING WITH
DESTINY

FREE GIFT!

**Find out how to tell your fortune
with our free pack of tarot cards this week!**

(Terms and conditions apply. Always read the small print.)

Oh yes, the wheel of fortune is turning my way again. Everyone's backing Raven's Cat Rescue Centre as our chosen charity.

Caspar was completely won over after our visit and so was Scott – he even offered to help out with the lighting on the film, so he's joined the *Lady and the Vamp* team!

Now that we're rehearsing after school I get to see Caspar almost every day. He always starts with a little 'motivational speech' inspired by his visit to Raven's house.

*'Let's do it for the abandoned.
The outcasts.
The shadow-walkers
The ones who dare to walk alone.
Let's do it for the black cats!'*

Then he winks at me and I know – just like *Lost Soul* predicted:

a. He's The One.
b. It's Meant To Be.

'I think he likes me!' I sigh to Starr after one of his speeches.

'You could be right,' she agrees. 'But I think there's someone else who likes you even more.' She nods her head towards Fat Nat who's hovering in the wings like a big, black bat.

'Oh no, not Nat,' I say impatiently as he gives us a little wave. 'He's just like a comedy vampire – a real pain in the neck. *Ha!*'

Starr's not amused. She thinks I'm being horrible but she doesn't understand – Nat's a lovely person but he's not the one for me.

After the rehearsal Caspar gets us all together because he's got some news. 'Ladies and gentlemen, I'm pleased to tell you that the date for filming is set for this Saturday and the location is the Goth capital—'

'Not Gotham City?' Nat shouts out. 'Will we meet Batman, too?'

Everyone laughs but Caspar carries on. 'We're going to Whitby – the place where Count Dracula himself arrived on a boat from Transylvania. He's the original batman – or should I say vampire-batman – so, who knows?'

Now everyone's bubbling with excitement and asking

thousands of questions. Caspar says that the school is providing a minibus and that he is also driving in his own 'Vladmobile'.

'Isn't it exciting – I can't wait!' I say to Starr on our way home. Scott's stayed behind to sort some technical stuff so it's just the two of us.

'Mmm,' Starr says, half-heartedly.

'Are you OK?' I ask.

'Sorry,' she says. 'I had some news this morning and I can't stop thinking about it...'

Ten minutes later we're sitting in a café sipping coffee.

'Take a look,' Starr says mysteriously as she hands over a sheet of folded glossy paper from her pocket.

I smooth it out and see that it's a page torn from *It's All About Me* – a magazine I used to buy.

(Mad's *note: Before I abandoned girl-world for Goth-world.*)

Suddenly Starr's face is smiling out at me and I scan the strapline:

Three Lucky Finalists In Our Cover Girl Competition

'*Omigoth*, what's all this about? You never told me you'd entered!'

'That's because I didn't know before today,' Starr says. 'Not till Honey phoned this morning. She sent my photo

in and now they want me to go to London for a fashion shoot!'

The way she says it you'd think she was being sent to the underworld or something but I'm really pleased for her.

'Starr – aren't you excited? This is your big break! It's your way into the fashion world, isn't it?'

She shrugs. 'You sound exactly like Honey. She says that if I get on the cover the next step will be to sign up with a modelling agency. Apparently you can do that even while you're still at school. She says I can model in the holidays and then – after I've made my name – I can step into fashion design from there.'

'Sounds like a good plan... Oh, not that I want you to move away. In fact that would be awful,' I add as the realisation of what this all means suddenly hits me.

'Exactly,' she says. 'Say I do win – then I'll *have* to move to London. Honey's got my future all mapped out for me.'

'Starr Child, the famous fashion icon! I always knew this would happen. Remember last year when you modelled in the School Fashion Show – it was obvious you had something special. Told you I'm psychic.'

'But it's not what I want!' Starr wails in frustration. 'You know that, Maddy. I don't want to be a walking dummy – and I'm not sure if I want to live with Honey, either. Yes, I love fashion but I want to *do* something with it. I don't know...design, or textiles, or—'

'But don't you think Honey's right – that this will open doors for you?'

'I don't know,' Starr says, picking up the paper again. 'It's been going round and round in my mind all day. You haven't got a crystal ball tucked away in your bag of tricks have you?'

'*Omigoth* – that's so spooky! *Lost Soul*'s got a fortune-telling special this week. No crystal balls, but it does have *Top Tarot Tips*! Look.'

I take out my mag and show her the page.

TOP TAROT TIPS

Tarot cards have dramatic pictures on them and each card has a special meaning. People have used them for hundreds of years to answer the BIG questions in life.

Follow our top tips to find out how...

'So, can you give me a reading?' she asks.

I feel a rush of Gothic-Goddess-style excitement. *Unleash the magic inside you* – that's what *Lost Soul* recommends. And if I learn to read the tarot cards I could find out my own fortune, too.

(Mad's note: Find out if I'm going to marry Caspar and have lots of little Gothlings.)

'Why not? Give me some time to read up on the *Top Tips* and come round later. Sneak a peek into the future with your friendly local fortune-teller, Lady Madalena Velvetcrush.'

She smiles and it's good to see her looking a bit more relaxed.

'Free of charge for best friends,' I add.

'OK, what time?'

'About eight o'clock? It's best if Max is in bed so we don't get disturbed.'

♡   ★   ♡

Of course nothing goes to plan in the Mad household.

I want to read up on tarot cards but when I get back, Mum's going out. Typical, she never goes out and now she chooses tonight of all nights to do it!

(*Mad's note*: My sixth sense must need recharging because I didn't see that coming.)

Then Dad says he's got urgent work to finish before an important meeting the next day, so I have to get Max ready for bed.

After his bath he wants his favourite story – all about huge, horrible hairy monsters. It would give any normal child nightmares! He loves it so much that I have to read it over and over before he drifts off to sleep.

So when Starr arrives five minutes later, my in-depth tarot study has only got as far as opening *Lost Soul* and glancing at the page.

TOP TAROT TIPS

Before you begin the exciting process of
tarot reading, make sure you study the cards
and their meanings.
Remember, you are dealing with something very
powerful and special…

'D'you really think this fortune-telling stuff works?' she
asks, picking it up and reading.

I look at the two packs of cards that came as free gifts.
At this point I should say I haven't read the *Top Tarot Tips*,
but I don't want to disappoint her. Starr's looking for
answers and I figure my sixth sense and Gothic Goddess
power can help her anyway, so it doesn't really matter.

'Pick a card and let's find out,' I say, shuffling the
smaller pack with the weird pictures because it looks more
interesting. I spread them out face down and wait for her
to choose.

'You have to pick three, right?' she says. 'Past, present
and future.'

I have no idea but she's obviously read it in *Lost Soul*
so I just nod and improvise, trusting the universe to
guide me.

And when I stare down at the first picture, which has
the word STAR printed on it, that's what happens.
Everything comes together and makes perfect sense…

'This is you,' I say, pointing to a woman sitting by water surrounded by a starry sky. 'You've been looking to the stars because you're searching for your Destiny. You know it's out there – you just have to find it.'

Then I pick up the second card. It's got an old-fashioned wheel on it with spokes spinning out from the centre. Underneath is printed THE WHEEL OF FORTUNE.

'And this is now,' I say, without even stopping to think because it feels so right. 'Your life is spinning round like a wheel and you feel as if it's turning upside down. You're confused but I sense that the Wheel of Fortune will stop turning soon.'

Then I pick up the last card. A tall building is on fire – it's been struck by a bolt of lightning and someone's falling from the window. Underneath is printed THE TOWER.

'This is your future,' I say, frowning because I can't quite see how it fits. There's something about it that's very disturbing. I look up to see Starr's frightened eyes fixed on mine. She's waiting to catch my words and I want to get it right.

I close my eyes, saying 'Just give me a second to concentrate.'

Now I'm wishing I'd read the *Top Tarot Tips* after all but it's too late. I've gone too far and if I stop now Starr will be more confused than ever. She needs my help and I must dig deep.

I think of Starr and what's best for her... What's her life's Fate? What does her future hold?

'You're going to make a big change in your life,' I say firmly, my eyes still shut. 'You're going to the photoshoot and you're going to win.'

And now I'm no longer sure if the cards are speaking to me or I'm making this up but I *do* know Starr and I'm convinced it can happen. She needs to live up to her name and find somewhere to shine.

I open my eyes and pick up the card, holding it out to Starr.

'Is that really what it means?' she whispers, tracing the picture with her fingertips.

'Yes,' I say. 'Look, the tower's been struck by lightning – that's you taking the fashion world by storm!'

'There's someone falling out of the tower...' She still sounds uncertain.

'One of your rivals – you're going to topple them all and win!'

And then it hits me that winning means she'll leave forever. I don't want her to go – she's one of my best friends. But this isn't about me, this is Starr's future. It's her Destiny and she might never get a chance like this again.

'But—'

'The tarot has spoken.' I pick up her cards and put them back in the pack. 'For the Highest Good of All, And It Harm None, So Be It.'

14

FINDING YOUR
LIFE PATH

Each of us has a Life Path –
a purpose and reason for being, which
our soul longs to express.

Are you on-course or are you
drifting off-track?
Take two simple steps to find your
way back...

It's late and I'm just dropping off to sleep, melting into shadows when the phone cuts in.

'Maddy?'

'Erm...yeah?'

'Sorry, were you asleep?'

'No,' I croak.

'You were, weren't you? Sorry – I called Honey again and we were talking for ages, I didn't realise it was so late... Anyway, I'd better tell you, I almost agreed to go to the fashion shoot, but there's a problem...'

'Yeah?'

'I have to go on Saturday...'

'But we're filming in Whitby on Saturday!' I sit up, suddenly awake.

'Exactly – and I can't let everyone down. I mean, it would affect you most of all because you're my substitute and—'

Step 1 Wishes can come true!

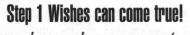

If you know where you want your life path to end – make a wish! Even if it seems a long way off, dreams can come true. As long as your motives aren't selfish...

For a moment I just can't speak. Me – play Juliet? Opposite Caspar? This is my Destiny. This is what I was born for! Maybe I'm still asleep? Maybe I'm dreaming...

'Starr, are you kidding? Of course I can take your part, don't worry about it. Follow your Destiny. Do what you have to do,' I squeak excitedly.

'But you'll have to learn all the words and—'

'You think I don't know them already? And you won't be letting anyone down, they'll understand.'

'Are you sure? It's strange, but once I found out I couldn't go to the shoot it made me more determined to try! Honey wants me to travel down tomorrow and get an early night so I'm fresh for Saturday morning. It'll mean missing school – she's going to phone and explain – but what can I say to Caspar and everyone?'

'Don't worry, leave it to me,' I say. 'And good luck, Starr – not that you'll need it!'

I put down the phone and smile.

You never know what surprises Fate has in store, do you?

♥ ★ ♡

So, after school the next day I find myself explaining what happened to Caspar, Scott and Nat.

'If Starr wins the competition she'll be the fashion face of next year! She's really sorry – but it's not her fault, is it? I mean who knows when Destiny will strike?'

Scott says nothing and Caspar's eyes spark with anger. Only Nat seems to take it well. 'Good luck to her, if that's what she wants to do,' he says.

'And while the lovely Starr pursues fame and fortune we are left with no leading lady,' Caspar storms. 'Well, that's it. The film's off.'

He turns to go and tell the others but I catch hold of his arm.

Step 2 Follow your life path

Visualise what you want and stay focused. Don't wait for someone to show you the way!

See it, feel it and make it happen...

'I can do it,' I say. 'That's what we agreed at the tryouts – remember? I know all the words. *Torn apart and no moment of bliss. Torn apart and no passionate kiss—*'

Caspar shrugs.

'And my hair's not black any more,' I say, yanking it from its band so it falls in loose curls, 'So I can play a normo now the dye's washed out.'

'I love red hair,' Nat says smiling.

'Auburn,' I correct him. 'And I'm sure we can find someone else to play my part. Juliet's mother doesn't get to say much, anyway.'

'Do I have a choice?' Caspar holds his hands up in despair. 'We can do the indoor scenes back at school but we've *got* to film the location scenes tomorrow. It's Whitby Goth weekend, the perfect setting. We can take some background shots of real Goths in the town and film the kiss scene in front of Whitby Abbey.'

'Meet Madalena Velvetcrush – the new leading lady,' Nat says, taking my hand and making a mock bow.

'Juliet to my Romeo,' Caspar agrees. As our eyes meet I can feel the universe turning – my Life Path is back on track.

'To the Vladmobile!' Nat cries, suddenly. 'Check out your transport for tomorrow, Lady Madalena.'

Both Nat and Caspar head out of the chapel and round the corner, but I hesitate. It's starting to drizzle and rain to me is like sunlight to a vampire.

'Here,' Scott says as he comes to my side and holds out an umbrella. 'Don't want a *hair-scare-nightmare*, do we?'

I smile. 'Thanks, Scott, you know me too well.'

'I do, or did. Not so sure about this new Gothic Goddess, though. And what's the deal with Starr? I thought—'

'*Omigoth!* What's that?' I say, suddenly distracted as we turn into the car park.

Ahead of us is a long, old-fashioned funeral car, complete with coffin in the back. Caspar and Nat are sitting in the front and a skeleton in a top hat is sitting up in the coffin behind them.

As we get closer we can hear haunting Goth-rock music playing from inside and when Caspar opens the door a haze of purple smoke billows out.

'Welcome to Caspar's Coffin Carrier, otherwise known as the Vladmobile,' he says grandly.

'We put the fun into funeral!' Nat adds.

'Cool special effects – is that the dry ice we were talking about?' Scott says, as we get into the hearse behind Caspar and Nat.

'Yes. The Vladmobile's a family heirloom. It's a long story,' Caspar says, starting the engine.

'Erm, is he a family heirloom too?' I point to the skeleton.

'Oh him – that's Rattlebones – he's got a part in the film. No relation, just a family friend.'

I settle back into the leather seats and admire the shiny coffin and polished silver and brass. It's all so *weird*! I'm in mobile Gothic heaven.

(Mad's note: *Other versions of paradise are also available.*)

Now I can't wait for my Gothic journey with Caspar tomorrow. Not only is it going to be an *über-Goth* extravaganza, but it's going to end with a kiss.

Our lips will meet and our souls will be joined forever.

It's written in the script and it's written in the stars. My Life Path stretches clear ahead of me...

And there's not a single obstacle in the way.

15

KISSING A
VAMPIRE

Whitby is amazing. It's *über-Gothic* – winding cobbled streets leading down to the silver sea. High on a cliff is the crumbling ruin of Whitby Abbey silhouetted against a stormy sky.

'It's Goth weekend,' Caspar tells us, 'when we descend on Whitby to celebrate our most Gothic festival – Halloween. The time of year when the spirits of the dead walk among us.'

As we drive into the town I'm amazed to see flocks of Goths everywhere. The streets are a riot of black-clad figures of all ages. There are whole families with identical long, black coats and clumpy black boots. I even see a dog in a batwing jacket!

So no one looks twice at our shiny hearse pumping out purple smoke and Goth-rock music. One or two give us a solemn nod of approval, but really we don't look out of place here – we belong.

Caspar parks the Vladmobile and I can't wait to get out and look at all the Goth clothes and crafts – but he has other ideas.

'I'm going to walk up to the Abbey and block out the moves,' he tells us. 'You can film some background shots of the streets and all things Gothic. Let's meet back here in about an hour.'

'How about we meet up in Dracula's Diner over there,' Nat says. 'Looks like it might rain again soon and I'm hungry.' He rubs his stomach. 'Nothing like a maiden sandwich and a pint of bat's blood to feed the soul.'

'But I'm a vegetarian vampire,' I protest.

'So ask for beetroot soup,' Scott says, laughing. 'Are you coming?'

Caspar's already stalking off down the street. 'No, you don't need me,' I say. 'You and Nat are the film crew – I'll just wander around and soak up the Goth-mosphere. Catch you later.'

2. Dracula – the most famous vampire of them all – is said to hang out in Whitby. Avoid it at all costs, especially the Abbey...

Of course, I do intend to catch up with them but – call it Fate, call it Destiny – my feet take me towards the Abbey instead.

Next thing I know I'm standing at the bottom of the cliff looking up at the one hundred and ninety-nine steps and wondering how far Caspar is ahead of me.

For once it's easy to play *Spot the Goth* because every other person in Whitby today is one! It's quite windy and as I trot up the steps, trying not to look too eager, lots of black coats and cloaks are flapping in the wind.

At last I spot a tall, *über-cool* Goth in front of me and I catch up with him, wishing I wasn't so red-faced and out of breath.

'Caspar – *phew* – what a coincidence,' I say casually, trying to keep up with him, which isn't easy when his long legs are taking two steps at a time.

3. Vampires can shapeshift at will. Look out for bats, rats and wolves. Oh, and canines with extra-long canines.

'Can you feel the black dog?' Caspar says, barely glancing at me. 'Can you feel it breathing down your neck?'

He reaches out and tickles the back of my head, which sends shivers of surprise down my spine.

'Erm, black dog?' I say, wondering if this is some kind of Goth code-word I don't know about.

'Yes, after Dracula's ship landed here in Whitby, he ran up these steps in the shape of a black dog,' Caspar says.

'Oh – I wonder if we should add black dogs to our charity fund,' I say stupidly. 'You don't see many of them around nowadays, do you?'

He doesn't reply and I'm too breathless to say anything else until we get to the top.

'*Whoo*, d'you think we could sit down for a minute?' I gasp, seeing some welcome benches ahead of us.

Caspar sits and I perch right next to him. I can't believe I've got him all to myself for the first time. This is the way it should be, this is our Destiny – and I feel sort of shy and reckless all mixed together.

4. Vampires can mesmerise you with their eyes. Avoid their hypnotic stare...

'Isn't it all too gorgeously Gothic up here?' I say, looking at the moss-covered gravestones, the old church and the ruined arches of Whitby Abbey rising up behind them.

'Are you really a believer?' Caspar asks, turning towards me. 'Madalena – have you truly embraced your dark side?'

His green and hazel eyes are flecked with gold – bold as a cat's and just as beautiful.

'Oh yes,' I say, pouting my black-lipsticked lips and wiggling my black, lacquered nails at him. 'I've truly embraced my dark side.'

He catches hold of my fingers and I nearly die right there and then – on a cliff top in front of a crumbling Gothic Abbey – because Caspar LeStrange is holding my hand.

'No, that's not what I mean. It's not about having black nails and lips. They are merely outward manifestations of the interior soul. It's about shunning the perky plastic side of life and plumbing the depths. You need to do this if you're going to show the transformation of Juliet Mortal for me.' And then he kisses my hand.

Omigoth!

I can barely breathe. The time is right and I know exactly what to say. 'I can transform myself,' I whisper. 'Let me prove it to you – let's practise now.'

'Good,' Caspar says. 'You are already playing the willing victim – just like Juliet. I like that. You need to get under your character's skin before we try acting a scene. Find your way into the part like I did with Romeo Diabolo.'

'How did you do that?' I ask. 'I mean, he's a vampire in your film but do you really believe in them?'

'It's Allhallows Eve, we're sitting in the churchyard in front of Whitby Abbey and a storm's brewing.' Caspar's gold-green eyes widen. 'What do you think – could the veil between this world and the spirit world be lifted? Could Dracula rise again?'

I look around me, at the gravestones, the wild, grey clouds and the ruined Abbey. Rain hangs heavy in the air like a silent threat and only one or two black-clad Goths brave the elements now.

I nod my head, wondering how I could I ever have had the slightest doubt.

---

5. Vampires like to hang out in graveyards. Sometimes upright, often upside down.

Caspar smiles his approval and continues. 'Romeo Diabolo is a lonely, solitary figure. A misfit, you could say. That's the key to his character – in many ways he's just like me.'

'But you've got lots of friends,' I protest.

Caspar dismisses my words with a wave of his black-gloved hand. 'I still live at the funeral parlour where I grew up. My mother was a make-up artist, my father an undertaker – she came to do some work for him and that's how they met – over a dead body.'

'Eeuuww!' Despite myself I can't help squirming at the thought. 'Oh, sorry,' I add, seeing a look of pain cross his face.

'That's the story of my beautiful-macabre life,' he says. 'I grew up with coffins and white lilies – I thought it was the norm, but at school I found out it was not. No one would come to my house to play, no one came to my birthday parties – I was the outcast, the weirdo.'

'Is that what made you become a Goth?' I ask.

He nods.

'You turned the bad things around and embraced your dark side!' I say in a flash of inspiration. 'And now you're a writer and a Gothic film-maker. That's so clever, it's Goth-genius.'

'Welcome to my world,' Caspar says, giving me a rare smile. 'Like Juliet you have to feel sympathy for Romeo locked in his demonic universe of vampires. His only wish is to find redemption with his soul mate and salvation in true love.'

'That's what I want too!' I say, wondering if he's been peering into my soul and reading my innermost thoughts. 'Er, me as Juliet, that is,' I add, as Caspar raises an eyebrow.

He nods. 'And as Juliet you have to be willing to kiss a vampire. You don't know what will happen – perhaps your love will free me, Romeo, from my dark side. Or perhaps you'll become one of the Undead, your restless soul roaming the world forever.'

It's starting to rain and thunder rumbles above us but I'm lost in the labyrinth of Caspar's words and the reflections in his eyes.

6. *It cannot be repeated too often. Kissing a vampire is not recommended, even if they do look good in black.*

He's a tortured soul, like me, and I'm the one who can save him. I remember my vision of us kissing high on a cliff – now it's time to risk everything.

I stand up and say the lines by heart, and they're no longer from Juliet to Romeo but from me to Caspar:

> *'Across wild lands and shifting seas*
> *My soul to your soul, I call out to thee –*
> *Romeo, Romeo wilt thou be mine*
> *And share my life till the end of time?'*

The wind's whipping my hair and snatching my words away but Caspar hears me. He stands at my side, sheltering me from the gathering storm, and answers my call:

> *'Juliet my love, my life, my breath*
> *Will you risk my kisses laced with death?'*

I look up at him.

'Yes,' I sigh, closing my eyes, as he moves towards me.

This is the moment I was born for. His lips brush mine in a butterfly kiss and then swoop down to my neck...

Ouch!

He bites.

16

THE
UNDEAD

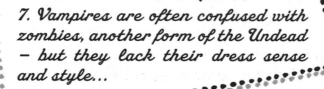
My eyes snap open in shock and I push Caspar away.

Anger flashes across his face and for a moment I wonder if he's mortal at all – or truly a vampire. Lightning forks the sky and that's when I see the fangs, gleaming white and sharp, caught in the illuminated moment.

Every horror movie I've ever seen flashes through my brain, the rain and wind lashing my thoughts into a frenzy of fear. Then thunder explodes above us and spurs me into action.

Spinning round I'm running away, down the one hundred and ninety-nine steps, slipping and sliding on the wet stones, almost crashing to my doom. Even at the bottom of the steps I don't stop running until I'm standing in front of Dracula's Diner, bent double with a side-splitting stitch, my breath ripping out in rags.

But the nightmare continues – a tall figure looms towards me out of the haze of raindrops, coat-tails flapping like a giant bat's.

Panic shoots through my veins like poison.

8. Vampires can move at tremendous speed and possess the strength of twenty men.

Wrenching open the door to the café I step inside – into the warmth, the light and the smell of hot food. I'm wet and bedraggled but I've escaped from a dark place back into the real world.

'Maddy, are you ok? You look like death warmed up!' Nat says coming over, tactful as ever.

'Bathroom. N…need to dry off,' I stutter.

'Sure,' he says and points to the back of the room where two doors are marked *Vampires* and *Vampirettes*.

'I'll order you a hot chocolate,' says Scott as he joins us. 'You look as if you need it.'

He's right, my teeth are chattering and I'm suddenly drained of all energy. In the bathroom I look at my pale, mascara-streaked face and wonder if I have indeed become Undead.

What just happened? The kiss with Caspar should have been the most romantic moment of my life but instead it was distorted into a Gothic nightmare.

I rinse my face with warm water and examine my neck, expecting to find two tiny holes where Caspar pierced my flesh, but there's nothing to be seen.

If only Starr was here, we could talk things through and make some sense out of it. But she's in London treading a different path towards her Destiny – to fame and fortune – and every minute is taking her further and further away.

At least Scott is outside and Nat was trying to be helpful too. I tell myself not to be so hysterical. OK, so Caspar will be in the café by now but what's he going to do in a room full of people? If I just make sure we're not alone together I'll be safe.

I open the bathroom door and step out into the crowded room. Scott and Nat are sitting at a table with the others but there's no sign of Caspar.

They make space for me and hand me a steaming mug of hot chocolate and some buttered toast.

'Change of plan, I'm afraid,' Nat says while I wolf down the toast. 'Caspar's been in – you just missed him. Apparently the Abbey is now closed to the public. There's a severe weather warning and it's not safe to go up there. After he came down the steps they were fenced off – and *No Entry* signs put up everywhere.'

'So what about the film?' I ask, sipping the hot chocolate and starting to feel human again.

'Cancelled. Caspar thinks we're cursed but there's no way we can do it in this weather. And if we want to get home today we need to set off now before it gets worse,' Scott says, getting up and putting his jacket on.

'We've been listening to the radio and it's not good – torrential rain, flooding and electric storms,' Nat explains.

He hands me my wet coat and helps me back into it, adding, 'Don't worry, Caspar's gone to get the Vladmobile, so we're in safe hands...'

❤   ★   ♡

The long, black car sweeps round to the front of Dracula's Diner. Scott piles into the back while Nat joins Caspar up front.

I hesitate for a moment – Caspar's Vladmobile is not exactly where I'd choose to be right now.

'Come on, Maddy, you're getting soaked out there!' Scott says. 'You'll catch your death of cold.'

'It's nice and warm in here,' Nat agrees.

They're my friends, I think. *They'll protect me if Caspar starts anything.* So I climb in.

It's not long before Scott's snoring quietly next to me but I'm still tense. The afternoon sky is dark and brooding – just like Caspar, who hasn't said a word. The mournful Goth-rock music adds to my unease, but after a while my eyelids feel so heavy that I can't help resting them. I'm just drifting off when I hear his voice.

'They both asleep in the back there?'

'Yeah, Maddy looked as though she needed it. She was a bit shaken up when she came into the café. Thunder gets some people like that, I suppose.'

'No, it was more than that. Do you know she stalked me up to the Abbey? I decided to give her a little acting lesson but she took it far too seriously – turned tail and ran off like a frightened rabbit.'

'What d'you mean *stalked* you?' Nat asks, voicing the words that flash through my mind at the same time.

My face flushes instantly – is that how he sees me? I remain as still as a corpse, desperate to hear more but dreading it at the same time.

'Oh come on, Nat. Maddy's a cute kid but she hasn't *stopped* stalking me since we started this project. I thought it was time to teach her a lesson and did my Dracula act. You know – right down to the fang-tastic kiss. The little Gothling was totally taken in by my charm and charisma. She knew Juliet's words off by heart – very sweet.'

'Yeah, but are you sure she knew you were acting?'

'Oh, she'll get over it. Anyway, thanks to the storm we'll have to film somewhere local this week instead of Whitby. I'm not happy about it but at least we'll get Starr back.'

'Poor Maddy, she really wanted that role. Can't you keep her as our leading lady?'

'No, Starr's got the perfect looks. She's my Juliet.'

'*Aah*, so you fancy her. Now I get it.'

'No, Nathaniel, my boy, I prefer someone my own age... Raven's the one who stole my heart. Why else d'you think I agreed to this cat charity charade? Who needs a Gothling when you can have a real Gothic Goddess?'

9. Vampires are cold, cruel and heartless beings incapable of loving anyone but themselves.

My head is pounding with the effort not to cry. Now I know our romantic cliff scene was nothing more than a joke to Caspar.

In fact *I'm* nothing but a joke.

A bad joke.

All my attempts to live up to his image and transform myself into a Gothic Goddess were ridiculous and I'm feeling sick to the pit of my stomach.

Suddenly the car lurches to a halt. 'Where are we?' Scott says, stretching and waking up.

'*Stop. Road ahead closed,*' Nat reads aloud. 'Looks like we'll have to take a diversion.'

I let out a half sob but when everyone looks at me I turn it into a sort of hiccup and yawn mixed together.

'You OK?' Scott says.

'Mmrmm,' I mumble, stretching my arms and muzzing

my hair to hide my face. Then I rummage around in my bag for a tissue and wipe away the tears that have sprung, quite suddenly, to my eyes.

With a few simple words Caspar has cast me adrift. Everything I've ever read in *Lost Soul* is coming back to haunt me and I don't know what to believe any more.

LIFE PATHS LOVE SPELLS Goddesses

Gothic magic Fate Free will Tarot

TELEPAHY SOUL MATES Stars Sixth sense

Why couldn't I see that the idea of Caspar falling for someone like me was as ridiculous as me believing he was a vampire?

...And yet he might as well be.

Why else would I feel like he's just ripped out my heart?

Why else would I feel like the Undead?

10. Do vampires and other paranormal beings exist? Check out the advertising feature on the next page...

17

SPOOK-HUNTERS:
INVESTIGATING THE
PARANORMAL

Lost Soul Advertising Feature

Spook-Hunters is a serious
organisation specialising in
paranormal investigation.
We operate a strict NO OUIJA
BOARD policy.

Read our Frequently Asked Questions
to find out more…

Nat switches on the radio, flicking between stations to see
if we can find out what's going on. When we catch the
end of the news the presenter's grave voice sends a chill
down my spine.

'…And finally the headlines.

✳ **Killer Storms are ripping across Britain, causing havoc. Electrical storms and torrential rain have caused transport chaos – leading to blocked roads and cancelled trains.**

✳ **Worst hit are London and the northeast coast of England, where trees and bridges have collapsed on roads and rail lines.**

✳ **You are advised not to travel today unless your journey is absolutely necessary.'**

'So what are we going to do now?' Caspar says, turning round to include us in the conversation.

'Looks like we'll have to stay here until we get the all-clear,' Scott suggests.

'What – spend the night in a dark lane – in a hearse – with a skeleton?' I squeak, getting more hysterical by the minute.

'I'm sure we passed a diversion sign further back up the road,' Nat says. 'Maddy's right – it's not very safe to stay here anyway. Look at those trees hanging over us – they don't look too steady. I vote we look for an alternative route and try to get back home.'

Luckily everyone agrees. We turn round and find the diversion sign. Then it's a slow crawl back home along flooded roads, stopping every now and again to move the odd fallen branch.

Scott and I had arranged to meet Starr in her flat above Bar Salsa when we got back, so I call her to say we'll be late but there's no reply.

'I just hope she makes it home OK,' Scott says when I tell him. 'Funny the storms hit Whitby and London the worst, isn't it?'

'Bad karma,' Nat agrees, which really gets me thinking.

Spook-Hunters
Frequently Asked Questions

a. Do storms increase paranormal activity?
b. Do our negative actions lead to heightened weather activity?

Answer:
Call Spook-Hunters now – these theories are currently under investigation.

All my dabbling in love spells and tarot – I know I didn't follow the rules too closely but at the time it didn't seem to matter. Now I'm worried.

Has my bad magic got anything to do with this bad weather?

My feet are wet and I'm shivering on the back seat in the dark, but that's not the only thing making me feel uncomfortable. I know I won't rest until we're safely home and Starr is too.

At last we reach the familiar streets of Westfield and I breathe a sigh of relief. Now all we have to do is meet up with Starr and my guilty conscience will vanish like a vampire at sunrise...

Suddenly I catch sight of a scrawled heading on a newspaper stand and my nerves start jangling all over again.

Rail network nightmare!

What if Starr's caught up in it?

I read her tarot only two days before and told her to travel to London – but what if I was wrong? What if the cards spelled out a warning?

There's still no response from her phone, so when we pull up outside Bar Salsa I can't get out of there quick enough.

'Thanks, bye!' I say, scrambling to get out as soon as we stop and running through the front door without a backward glance.

We aren't supposed to go into the bar at all. There is a back door but I know that even if Starr is in upstairs you can't hear the bell with the TV on and it'll takes ages for anyone else to get to it. This is an emergency and I worm my way through the crowd to get to the bar.

Scott catches me up and we can see that Matt's busy serving drinks. We have to shout together to be heard. 'Where's Starr?'

'Not home yet but is definitely coming back tonight,'

Matt says, looking too frazzled to worry about it.

'She told me she'd walk up from the station when her train gets in,' he adds before getting back to his customers. 'I'll tell her you came round.'

We don't want to worry him but both Scott and I know that Starr's train was due back hours ago.

She's late.

Very late.

As soon as we get outside I start to panic. It's been a long, tiring, upsetting day and I feel like I'm hallucinating. I can't get that final Tarot card out of my mind – the tower struck by lightning, the body tumbling out of the window. What did it mean?

'Omigoth, Scott, d'you think Starr's OK? What if a tree fell on the line or a bridge collapsed or—'

'Maddy, calm down, will you? Let's go to the train station and get some hard facts,' Scott says, bringing me back to earth but not for long...

Spook-Hunters
Frequently Asked Questions
What manifestations are investigated?

Answer:
Ghosts, spirits, ectoplasm, orbs, disembodiment, astral bodies, phantasms and much, much more...

The rain eases off a bit and because it's Halloween lots of people are walking around dressed up in the most bizarre outfits.

This doesn't exactly help my grip on reality. We make our way through groups of witches, skeletons, monsters and devils carrying pumpkins with glow-in-the-dark grins. It's all so *weird* and *nightmarish that I feel as if real evil spirits are walking the streets* tonight.

At the station Scott asks about Starr's train and the man at the information desk looks grim.

'Sorry, all trains are delayed due to the weather,' he says, stating the obvious. Then he disappears into the back office and speaks into his walkie-talkie to find out more.

I think I catch the word 'incident', but he doesn't mention it when he comes back out again. 'Looks like they've laid on some buses to take people to their stations,' he smiles. 'If she's lucky she may have got on one of those. Why don't you grab yourselves a coffee and wait for more news?'

By now I feel completely spooked and I can't fight the growing sense of panic inside me.

'*Omigoth, omigoth*, I've got a bad feeling about all this,' I mutter as we take our drinks over to a table by the window. 'I'm sure that man was hiding something.'

'Maddy, think positive. Worrying won't help,' Scott says.

'But it's all my fault. You were right! I shouldn't have dabbled in the dark arts,' I blurt out. 'The storms, the lightning... It's me – I caused cosmic chaos!'

'Maddy, people are looking, keep your voice down!'

But I can't. Seeing the newspaper weather warnings in black and white has hit home and the words are tumbling out in a sudden urge to confess all.

'I broke the rules, Scott. I did a...well, a freestyle love spell and the universe is angry, which is why the weather's so freaky—'

'Maddy, you don't control the universe! These storms were forecast days ago!'

Scott's got a point but it's no use. I'm in full flow, just like the rain streaming down outside the window.

'Then I told Starr's future in the tarot. I did it for the best but I should have followed rules – the Top Tarot Tips!' I wail, as everyone puts down their tea cups and stares.

'Instead I made it up and meddled with magic. Now I've caused bad karma! What if the tower card was a warning and I should have told Starr? What if her train was hit by lightning and crashed? What if I've killed my best friend? *Aaaggghhhh!*'

I stand up suddenly and my chair clatters to the floor.

'It's a ghost!'

Everyone goes quiet as I raise my shaking finger and point at the window. A deathly pale face is pressed up against the glass, its hair hanging down in dark ribbons. The eyes are black holes, streaked and smeared with tear stains and shadows and they're staring, staring.

It's a distorted nightmare vision of someone I once knew so well...

'Starr – *nooo!* She's come back to haunt me for what I've done!' I scream into the stunned silence.

I stand there for the tick of two heartbeats unable to move.

Suddenly the face disappears.

Then Scott starts laughing, closely followed by everyone else...

Spook-Hunters
Frequently Asked Questions
Do ghosts really exist?

Answer:

To find out if you have seen a ghost, ghoul or other paranormal phenomenon, please call our investigators on **01211 0001** or check out our website: **www.spook-hunters.r.i.p.uk**

18

AGONY
HEALER

Of course, when Starr walked into the café, dripping wet but very much alive, I have never been so embarrassed in all my life.

Eternal embarrassment till the end of time. In fact, whenever you read this, wherever you are, I'll still be blushing…

It turns out that Starr's bus dropped her back at the station and she'd spotted us as she walked past the café.

At least she *thought* it was us – the rain was so bad that she had to press her face right up against the window to get a better look.

The sight of her rain-soaked, mascara-streaked face has turned me off Gothic-magic forever. I really think I put her life in danger with my fake tarot readings and freestyle spells.

When we went back home with her I confessed everything. Starr was totally cool about it – she told me she didn't believe the tarot reading but it made her think again. She went to London to find out how it would feel if she did actually win. And guess what – she did!

Starr was cool about that, too, even though all three judges picked her as their first choice! They said she was a natural and that she had that extra special something you're simply born with.

'It's like you said, Maddy, I feel like Fate is trying to tell me something – or at least my darling mother is – and I've finally given in. Honey thinks I need to move to London now I've won the competition. Apparently there's an agency already interested. Don't say anything to Matt though. I haven't told him yet,' she looks down before we can catch the expression in her eyes.

I can guess what she's thinking – it's not going to be easy to tell her dad she's leaving. Destiny is a hard taskmaster. If Starr is going to follow her dream it means leaving Westfield, her dad and her friends. I'm going to miss her so much but I'm really happy for her too.

Unlike me, she's found her true Life Path and she's on her way!

So, this week has been *über-yuck*, to say the least. In one day I lost one of my best friends and the love of my life. Now I'm just going through the motions – like a braindead zombie.

Everything seems pointless and I've lost my mojo.

(Mad's note: Well, actually I haven't – I still carry my love-spell mojo around with me in the vain hope that it might work. See note below.*)

To make things worse I've seen Caspar every day since then. First we had to film *Lady and the Vamp* in the school grounds and after that we all met to sort out the Goth-up day and Gala night.

I'm still not over him.

Every time I see him, hear him or accidentally brush against his crushed-velvet cloak, it's torture and I die a thousand deaths.

Even though his cruel words drove a stake through my heart at Whitby I can't stop loving him. He's so clever and creative and Goth gorgeous. None of that's changed, so it seems that my true love for him will never die...

(*Mad's note: Love minus Hope = über-pain.)

Anyway, at least everyone entered into the spirit of the Goth-up and Cough-up day today and it was a total success. I've never seen so much black velvet, silver jewellery, eyeliner and fake tattoos – and that was just the teachers!

So here we are after school counting all the money we've made for the Black Cat Charity, Scott, Starr and me, huddled round the desk like three witches.

'*When shall we three meet again – in thunder, lightning, or in rain?*' Scott croaks as we scoop up the last of the coins into plastic money bags.

'In two hours it's the Goth film night,' I reply, 'and when it's all over I'm going to banish black from my life forever. It's goodbye Gothic Goddess for me.'

I continue scooping the piles of coins into bags but the other two stop dead and stare at me as if I've grown two heads.

'So what's going to happen to Madalena Velvetcrush?' Scott asks.

'And what's a wardrobe without stylish black?' Starr adds.

I shrug. 'Maybe it's just not my colour. Ever since I walked in the shadows bad things have happened—'

'How can you say that?' Scott asks. 'It looks like we've made a fantastic sum of money for the Black Cat Charity already and we've sold out of tickets for tonight, too.'

'Yes, just think how happy Raven will be when we present her with a massive cheque,' Starr agrees.

At the mention of Raven's name I can't help feeling my old *Jealousy Junkie* twinges and I'm sure my face has turned sickly green. Caspar asked if he could bring Raven as his special guest of honour tonight. Now I know how much he likes her, I'm not looking forward to seeing them together at all.

'Hmm,' I mumble, lapsing into Gothic Gloom. 'I still don't think that casting love spells and forecasting the future was any use at all. Nothing worked and I think it caused more harm than good.'

'Yes, but remember when you told us you had a vision about cats and this Gala Film Night?' Starr says. 'If you hadn't foreseen that, we wouldn't be here now, would we?'

'And Starr wouldn't be going off to London to start her glittering career if you hadn't tinkered with the tarot,' Scott agrees. 'Your prediction gave her the kick-start she needed.'

'Yes, I suppose—'

'Well, actually, I've decided to turn the offer down,' Starr says quietly.

Now it's my turn to look shocked.

'But it's your Destiny. You can't fight Fate,' I say, trotting out the lines I've read over and over in my magazines.

'That's what I thought. That's what I told Matt, too, and he was brilliant about it,' Starr says. 'He wished me luck and told me to do what I had to do, then he disappeared into his room and started strumming his guitar – he always does that when he's upset—'

'So you changed your mind because of him?' I ask.

'No, no it wasn't that. I went into my room and started to pack a few things straightaway because I was feeling so wired. But when I took down my suitcase it was like I was watching myself from high above in a little corner in the room... And I thought *This isn't me. I don't want to do this. I want to stay here. At home. With my dad. With my friends...'*

'But Starr, you've got that extra special something. Even the judges said so,' I argue back, because – much as I want Starr to stay – I'd hate her to waste what she's got. I used to be jealous of her because of it but now she's my friend and I want the very best for her.

'Hang on a minute – Starr does have a right to say no here,' Scott says. 'There is such a thing as Free Will, you know.'

'Moving to London is Honey's Destiny, not mine,' Starr says, simply. 'You know she always regretted giving up modelling when she had me – I can't live my life for her.'

'But it's one of those fork-in-the-road moments!' I say.

Scott looks blank, so I explain. 'Sometimes Fate adds an unexpected twist to your Life Path. You have to choose which way to go and it will make a big difference. I read it in *Lost Soul.'*

'And your point is?' he asks, still looking blank.

'Starr, what if you've chosen the wrong fork? You might never get a chance like this again.'

'Then I'll take the risk. All I know is that now is not the right time. It doesn't mean I'm giving up on fashion, Maddy. I still want to get into design but I'm going to work at it my way. Matt said the harder you work, the luckier you get. So maybe Fate will give me another break some time.'

'Yeah,' I sigh, feeling suddenly in awe of Starr and her willpower. 'I wish I was as strong as you...'

'Oh for goodness' sake – you're not still moping about Caspar are you?' Scott says impatiently.

I can't answer him. My eyes fill with tears and I hang my head in shame. 'I know it's ridiculous and I know it'll never happen,' I blurt out, speaking to the table instead of them. 'But I can't shake off the idea that he's the one for me. It's ever since I read it in my stupid stars... Oh, I wish I'd never meddled in all this stuff and I wish I'd never picked up that first copy of *Lost Soul*!'

'Um, talking of *Lost Soul* – did you buy this week's issue?' Scott asks.

I shake my head. 'No...never want to see it again,' I mutter.

'Oh, well, I bought it for you,' Scott says. 'And there's something in it I was hoping you'd read. Er...it's in the *Lad Mag Pull-Out* on the problem page.'

I look up to see him fishing the mag out of his school bag. Scott hates my trashy mags and the fact that he's actually bought one is very disturbing. It's as if the whole universe has turned upside down.

He opens it up and spreads it out on the desk. Then he pushes it towards me but my eyes are still blurry and I can't focus.

'Shall I read it?' Starr asks gently.

I nod and she begins.

Dear Agony Healer,

My best friend has always been a mag-hag but recently she got addicted to your Gothic number. Since reading that love is in the air she's been obsessed with a certain Goth Guy. She's taken drastic steps to transform herself into a Gothic Goddess, bending all the rules of magic in a bid to get this guy to notice her.

In my opinion he's an arrogant show-off and is enjoying the attention. He reminds me of Dracula collecting his many brides.

Anyway, I don't believe in all this Gothic Magic stuff myself but I can't help thinking she's heading for a fall. She's changed so much recently I hardly know her but she's still my best friend and I don't want to see her get hurt.

She probably won't listen to me but she does read problem pages all the time, so I'd be grateful if you could print this along with your advice...

From
Scientific Scott

'*Omigoth*, I can't believe you actually wrote to *Lost Soul*!' I say, not sure whether to be angry at Scott for publicising my problems or touched by his concern.

He nods. 'Sorry, it seemed the logical thing to do.'

'So what was the reply?' I add, curiosity winning out over everything else.

Starr picks up from where she left off:

Dear Scientific Scott,
You are right to be worried about your friend.
Just like vampires, some people can drain your energy and life force away. It sounds like this Goth guy is having a negative effect on her and she's losing her true soul, which is very unhealthy.
Science and Magic have more in common than you think. They are both powerful transformational forces.

Combine the two and I can confidently predict that you will figure out a way to help your friend...
Good luck!
Agony Healer

'Um, thanks for taking the trouble, Scott,' I say, sinking back into my pit of self-pity, 'but my head already *knows* Caspar's no good for me. It's just my heart that won't listen...'

Starr puts her arm round me, which makes my eyes go blurry again. 'It's hopeless,' I add in true Gothic gloom, 'and that stuff about science and magic makes no sense at all.'

'But it does. I've worked it out – it's all a question of looking at things logically.'

'Yeah, right,' I sigh, thinking that Scott just doesn't get it at all. 'So what do you suggest? *Write down all Caspar's positives and negatives on a piece of paper and add them up with a calculator?*'

'Magic,' Scott replies.

'Magic?' Starr and I both chorus in amazement.

(Mad's note: This from the guy who said magic is nothing but superstition and speculation!)

'Yes, I've analysed the problem scientifically and come to the obvious conclusion.'

'Meaning?'

'Meaning you've got to cast a *Reverse Love Spell*.'

19

REVERSE
LOVE SPELL

Golden Rules of Spelling

Remember, love spells are only as powerful as the amount of belief and energy you put into them...

'No, no, no, no, definitely not,' I say, shaking my head. 'No more meddling with magic. I'm finished with all that and I'm surprised you'd even suggest it. You don't even believe in it anyway, do you?'

'But *you* do,' Scott says, avoiding the question. 'And that's what matters. You cast a love spell on Caspar but it rebounded back three times as strong! You're hopelessly in love, you said so yourself. So you need to perform a *Reverse Love Spell* to neutralise its effects.'

'No more Gothic Magic. I'm done with all that. It messes with your mind and...I wouldn't know what to do, anyway,' I finish lamely.

'Well if you change your mind, there are some helpful hints in *Lost Soul* this week,' Scott says, tucking the mag into my bag.

'Now we'd better get sorted for tonight,' he adds, checking his watch. 'Time's running out.'

Despite my desire to give up on all things Gothic, I have to admit that the school hall is transformed by the time we put the finishing touches to it.

The tables are covered in black crepe paper, scattered with silver moons and stars, and set with a large white candle and a vase of white lilies. On the walls are large, ornate mirrors (provided by Raven), artistically draped with clouds of cobwebs.

It's a dazzling mix of decadence and decay – *über-perfect*!

Nat's in charge of catering and has concocted a purple berry juice called *Gothic Sunset* and a red berry juice called *Dracula's Delight*.

Caspar has already set up the film equipment and he's gone to pick up Raven in his Vladmobile. We've put a red carpet down the school steps at the main entrance and actors from the film are being Goth-greeters to show people the way.

Max is too young to come but my parents found a poor unsuspecting victim to baby-sit, so they'll be there. We've put them at the same table as Scott's mum, Hyacinth, and Starr's dad, Matt. I wonder if they know what over-the-top Goth treats are in store!

Five minutes before Caspar is due to arrive I retreat to the Vampirettes' room to fix my make-up and check that I look OK.

I'm wearing my *Lady and the Vamp* costume again – the one with the flattering scoop neck. Starr's pinned my hair up and I've chosen matching silver cobweb drop-earrings, ring and bracelet.

As I look into a mirror to apply my black lipstick I can see that sleepless nights spent crying into my pillow have left me pale-faced with shadows under my eyes. Seeing my hollow cheeks makes me think of the problem page description of Caspar as a vampire draining my energy and life force.

(Mad's note: Oh the cruel irony of life – just as I'm ditching the Dark Side I'm looking effortlessly über-Goth!)

In fact old Goth habits die hard, and I snatch five minutes to read through *Lost Soul*. The *How to Reverse a Love Spell* guide is especially interesting – not that I'm going to try it, of course.

'Time to go out front and do some Goth-greeting,' Nat says as I head back to the hall. We follow him out just as everyone starts arriving. Then, in the distance, we hear a blast of Goth-rock music...

The Vladmobile cruises up to the bottom of the steps billowing purple smoke, scattering Goths in its wake.

Rattlebones doesn't move but Caspar leaps out of the driving seat like a bat out of hell. His hair is slicked back, showing his strong cheekbones and shining eyes. He looks so Goth-damn-gorgeous that my Undead heart kicks back into life and I fall for him all over again. Then he opens the passenger door with a flourish of his red silk-lined cloak and out steps Raven.

There's a sharp intake of breath from the crowd as she stands up looking like a vision from the underworld. She's wearing a black whale-boned corset offset with black feathers and she throws back her shiny black and purple hair (how can extensions look so natural?) to reveal marble-white shoulders. Her lacy black skirt flows down to ankle boots and she's carrying an antique black parasol in her elegant black-gloved hands.

Even I have to admit that together they make a perfect match, and everyone claps as Caspar plays to the crowd and bows to kiss her hand.

So, my vision of the Goth-tastic couple on the carpet has come true, but not in the way I expected. That romantic gesture hurts – how is it possible to love someone so much and not be loved in return?

Caspar escorts Raven up the red carpet and when the lights go off silent tears stream down my face. I can hardly focus on the film – except to register how stunning Starr looks as Juliet Mortal and how fiendishly handsome Caspar is as Romeo Diabolo.

Everyone gasps and laughs in all the right over-the-top Goth places but as soon as it ends I scuttle away before the lights go up to reveal my blotchy face. The applause is still ringing in my ears as I sneak outside to mope in true Goth-style.

It's good to be alone – the night air is cool on my face and I sit on a school bench and look up at the sky. A pale, crescent moon is fading like my hopes for true love with Caspar, and something in that image releases me.

Scott's right – I have to let go.

I call upon the power of my Gothic Goddess. She never really went away despite what I said about giving up on her. I don't need to wear black to prove it, but a part of me will always be *Glad To Be Goth*. After all what is day without night, sunshine without shadows and eyes without eyeliner?

My shadow self will always walk with me and I'm grateful to Caspar for giving me a glimpse of the Dark Side.

So here, alone at night, under a crescent moon, I feel ready to cast the perfect *Reverse Love Spell*. And I know exactly what to do...

♥ Reverse Love Spell ♥

Best performed under a waning moon, feel free to improvise using the principles of magic you've learned so far.

What matters most is the energy and feeling you put into it.

Remember to walk widdershins – anticlockwise – to undo the effects of a previous spell.

My bare hands dig into the earth and when the hole is deep enough I reach into my bag for the love-spell mojo I could never throw away. Now it's the central ingredient in my leave-taking ritual – I place it in the earth and cover it with soil, pressing down firmly.

Then I walk around it widdershins, speaking the Reverse Love Spell that has formed in my mind since reading *Lost Soul* earlier:

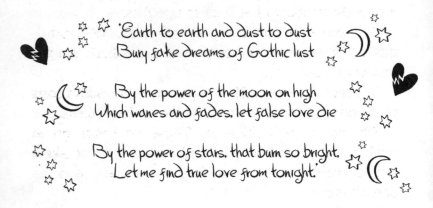

'Earth to earth and dust to dust
Bury fake dreams of Gothic lust

By the power of the moon on high
Which wanes and fades, let false love die

By the power of stars, that burn so bright,
Let me find true love from tonight.'

Finally the special words to seal the spell safely:

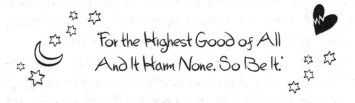

'For the Highest Good of All
And It Harm None. So Be It.'

Just as I finish a voice behind me makes me jump.
'*Maddy!* I've been looking for you everywhere.'

I hold my breath.

Is this it? After all my bungled bad magic have I made True Magic at last?

A heartbeat later I turn to find myself looking at a dark figure silhouetted against the light.

'Who...who is it?' I whisper.

'Oh, sorry, it's only me, Nat. Here, I brought you this – *Dracula's Delight*.' He steps forward holding out a blood-red drink. It's got a black straw poking out of it and a comedy cardboard bat stuck to the glass.

'Oh, you gave me a shock! I thought...well, um... thanks,' I take the drink from him and step back into the real world again.

'You should come in. They're giving out the Goth Oscars soon and I bet you'll be up for an award,' he explains.

'Oh, no, I don't think so. S'pose I'd better go in though. Mum and Dad will wonder where I am.' I take a step forward but he's standing in the way and he doesn't move.

'Um, there was another reason why I was looking for you,' he says in a gruff, serious voice I haven't heard before.

I'm so glad it's dark out here and he can't see my face, which is turning the same colour as my drink. I don't need a crystal ball to guess what's coming next.

He clears his throat and tries again. '*A-hem*, now the film's over, I realised that we won't be seeing so much of each other. Well, except in school that is, but that's not the same as...er... Anyway, I wondered if...y'know, we could go out together some time?'

I can hear the ice clinking in his glass as he fiddles nervously with his straw. It's really cost him to say all this and I can't help respecting him for that. Poor Nat, he's such a lovely person – I just wish he was my type!

He feels the same way about me as I do – sorry, *did* – for Caspar and I don't want him to be treated the way I was. How can I let him down gently without hurting his feelings?

'Nat – um…maybe we could meet up some time—'

'Yeah?' I hear the hope in his voice and instantly regret what I just said. It feels like Fate is playing this huge practical joke on me, only I'm not laughing.

You wanted true love, it's saying, *well, here you are.*

'Yes, we could see each other as friends,' I explain.

'Oh, yes, of course,' he hesitates. 'But I didn't mean…' He stops and takes a sip of his drink. '*Er*…d'you think we could forget what I just said? Stupid, really, must be this *Gothic Sunset* going to my head. All that sugar. *Friends*, yes, that's great…'

He moves towards the steps and I start thinking how weird it is that two seconds after I wished for true love, Nat appeared. Other lines from other spells come back to me now:

Whisper love spells to the air
So they will carry everywhere
One alone your words will hear
One alone will then draw near...

I follow him across the grass and think how it's so unfair. He's funny and kind but he just doesn't do it for me. If only he was like... Something makes me stop here because I know Caspar's name doesn't fit anymore. The Caspar I thought I loved doesn't even exist...

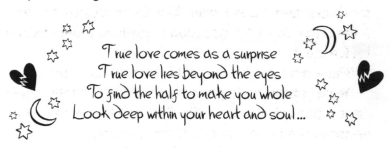

True love comes as a surprise
True love lies beyond the eyes
To find the half to make you whole
Look deep within your heart and soul...

Nat climbs the steps ahead of me. He's nearly at the entrance – this is my last chance to call him back.

Fate has thrown one of those forks-in-the-road right at me.

Which way shall I go?

I don't know – this isn't a happy ending like those Five-Minute-Fiction stories you read in magazines. This is real life and I'm confused.

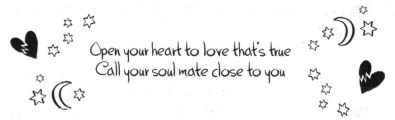

Open your heart to love that's true
Call your soul mate close to you

'I'm confused,' I say out loud.

'Why?' Nat stops. 'Is it my fault? I'm sorry, I didn't mean—'

'No, no, it's not that. I've made a complete fool of myself recently over...well, Count Dracula in there,' I say.

'Once bitten, forever smitten?' he smiles.

'Not any more,' I smile back. He's got a nice smile – it's catching. 'But it's left me feeling messed up and...that's why I said we should see each other as friends. I don't think I can cope with anything else. Not now, anyway, but I really would like to meet up...if you still want to?' I add uncertainly.

'*We-ell,*' he says, hesitating, and I'm sure he's going to say no. That would be just typical of my luck at the moment...

'Oh, go on then, if you insist.' He comes back down and holds out his arm. 'Care to join me?'

So, here's a vision I didn't foresee – Madalena Velvetcrush accompanying Fat Nat, the smiley Goth, up the red carpeted steps.

Out of the dark and into the light.

ISSUE 1

Maddy

JEALOUSY JUNKIE

Sneak Preview

WHAT'S IN THE FIRST ISSUE OF MADDY?

Cringes, confessions and caught-on-camera clangers!
A True Confessions special

Maddy and Scott meet Starr for the first time...

What do you do when you fall out with your best friends?

ISSUE 3

Maddy

DESSERT DIVA

WHAT'S IN THE NEXT ISSUE OF MADDY?

Maddy's recipe for romance!
Another True Confessions special

Scott and Starr stir up trouble — find out how...

Fit and fabulous!
Top tips for the chocolatey-challenged

More Orchard books you might enjoy

Clarice Bean, Don't Look Now	Lauren Child	978 1 84616 507 8
Clarice Bean Spells Trouble	Lauren Child	978 1 84362 858 3*
Utterly Me, Clarice Bean	Lauren Child	978 1 84362 304 5*
The Truth Cookie	Fiona Dunbar	978 1 84362 549 0*
Cupid Cakes	Fiona Dunbar	978 7 84362 688 6
Chocolate Wishes	Fiona Dunbar	978 1 84362 689 3*
Clair de Lune	Cassandra Golds	978 1 84362 926 9
Secrets, Lies and My Sister Kate	Belinda Hollyer	978 1 84616 690 7*
The Truth About Josie Green	Belinda Hollyer	978 1 84362 885 9
Hothouse Flower	Rose Impey	978 1 84616 215 2
My Scary Fairy Godmother	Rose Impey	978 1 84362 683 1
Shooting Star	Rose Impey	978 1 84362 560 5
Forever Family	Gill Lobel	978 1 84616 211 4*
Seventeen Times as High as the Moon	Livi Michael	978 1 84362 726 5
Do Not Read This Book	Pat Moon	978 1 84121 435 1
Do Not Read Any Further	Pat Moon	978 1 84121 456 6
Do Not Read Or Else	Pat Moon	978 1 84616 082 0

All priced at £4.99, except for those marked * which are £5.99.
Clarice Bean, Don't Look Now is £6.99.

Orchard Red Apples are available from all good bookshops, or can be ordered direct
from the publisher: Orchard Books, PO BOX 29, Douglas IM99 1BQ
Credit card orders please telephone 01624 836000 or fax 01624 837033or visit our
website: www.orchardbooks.co.uk or email: bookshop@enterprise.net for details.

To order please quote title, author and ISBN and your full name and address.
Cheques and postal orders should be made payable to 'Bookpost plc.'
Postage and packing is FREE within the UK
(overseas customers should add £1.00 per book).

Prices and availability are subject to change.